THE ENDLESS SUMMER

Translated from the
Danish by Gaye Kynoch

THE
ENDLESS
SUMMER

a requiem

MADAME NIELSEN

OPEN LETTER
LITERARY TRANSLATIONS FROM THE UNIVERSITY OF ROCHESTER

Copyright © Claus Beck-Nielsen, 2014
Translation copyright © Gaye Kynoch, 2018
Originally published in Denmark as *Den Endeløse Sommer*

First edition, 2018
All rights reserved

Library of Congress Cataloging-in-Publication Data: Available.
ISBN-13: 978-1-940953-69-4 | ISBN-10: 1-940953-69-3

*This project is supported in part by a grant from
the Danish Arts Foundation.*

DANISH ARTS FOUNDATION

*This project is supported in part by an award from the National Endowment
for the Arts and the New York State Council on the Arts with the support of
Governor Andrew M. Cuomo and the New York State Legislature*

ART WORKS.
arts.gov

NEW YORK
STATE OF
OPPORTUNITY.

**Council on
the Arts**

Printed on acid-free paper in the United States of America.

Text set in Bodoni, a serif typeface first designed by
Giambattista Bodoni (1740–1813) in 1798.

Design by N. J. Furl

Open Letter is the University of Rochester's
nonprofit, literary translation press:
Dewey Hall 1-219, Box 278968, Rochester, NY 14627

www.openletterbooks.org

THE
ENDLESS
SUMMER

The young boy, who is perhaps a girl, but does not yet know it. The young boy, who is perhaps a girl, but will never touch a man, never strip naked with a man and rub skin against his skin, never ever, no matter how titillatingly repellant the notion might be. The young boy, this fetching young boy with the delicate features, the big eyes, and the huge anxiety for war and illness, for body, sex, and death.

It begins with a boy, a young boy, who is perhaps a girl, but does not yet know it. The young boy, so fetching, so delicate, so tender, so shy, plays guitar in a band. They're playing at a party for a crowd of young people they don't know, and who don't know them, and it's their first gig, and it's that very evening. (And later, first the girl comes, and then, but just in a glimmer, like a shadow, a dazzling shadow, a shadow of light, the mother, then the two little brothers, who climb up the walls, on the shelves and on the cupboards in the dark rooms in the basement under the farmhouse where she has withdrawn in order to escape the stepfather's eyes, his sickly nasal voice, his gun and his inferiority and hatred of every woman, fear he disguises as disdain, and where she now lives, the girl, in the basement, the walls papered with posters of Paul Young, who is still young and beautiful and soft in the pictures and later, very soon, will be fat and alcoholic and, following a swift and efficient downward spiral, will die, and then, like an epiphany, a dazzling light, the mother, her aristocratic figure, the long gracious limbs and strong bones, the sleek ivory-colored hair flowing down her back, the stallion she rides in the mist rising off the early summer morning fields seen through one of the small grimy window panes in the basement where he has just stirred and propped himself up on one elbow under the duvet in the damp warmth of the girl's languid body, the girl who is still asleep at his side, the dark round and soft girl with the delicate bones and big soft breasts, the eternally languid pleasure-lover and the aristocratic fair Nordic mother, her straight back and the steamy breath from the horse's slimily-soft nostrils, and then, with no warning, the stepfather, one morning, alone in the big rustic kitchen, the slender young boy and the stepfather who sits down opposite him and starts talking about weapons, guns and pistols, and especially the bullets and particularly the dumdum bullets, their magic effect, the almost invisible hole in the flesh, just here, right in the solar plexus where the bullet enters, almost without leaving a trace, and at the very moment it penetrates the darkness it explodes its way out and leaves the back, or what once was a back, one big ragged bleeding crater, the stepfather's story about the bullets and the girl's about the detectives paid by the stepfather to follow the mother everywhere as soon as she turns out of the avenue and is out of sight (and out of shooting range), and who clean him out so that he, who just a few years ago along with his older brother Buller inherited everything from their father and from one day to the next became a multimillionaire and bought an estate in Jutland, a magnificent manor house with sixteen toilets and bathrooms, can now hardly afford gas for his second-hand car, the detectives, who he, the young boy, never sees at all, albeit their shadows fall around him in the empty rooms when he walks through the house on his own, not a word, even though everyone except the two little brothers knows about their existence, quite openly, like a religious taboo everyone simply accepts as a matter of course, the mother and her daughter and the stepfather who knows that they know but doesn't let it affect him, doesn't try to hide anything, as if the terror is even more deadly from being obvious and unmentionable, and as if the mother's aristocracy, her untouchability, is even more supreme from her getting on with life, her daily round, as if nothing has happened, which just makes the stepfather's hatred and desperation and inferiority and obsession even greater and more bombastic, it consumes him, with every day he grows paler and thinner and savagely embittered, and determined it will be over his dead body that he lets go of this woman, lets her go free, even if it will consume him, and it will, but not now, first he'll just disappear, one day he's suddenly gone, and the summer has started, an endless summer, in which nothing happens, in which he, the slender boy, falls out of the world, the world he came from, and into this other world, which is a world in itself, where time and light stand still and the dust rotates and no one does anything, nothing other than living as if they were in a different era and a completely different location, as if the white farmhouse is a governor's residence on St. Croix in the final days of the empire when everything is too late and thus suddenly at last possible. The mother spends her days on the back of her stallion and doesn't come in until darkness falls, and she sits in the kitchen with a glass of wine, surrounded by candles, and the girl and the young boy stay in bed until late in the afternoon and never get properly up, but wander around the house wearing one another's clothes, the young boy dressed like a yet to be sexed toreador or a virgin, and sit in the kitchen and drink milky coffee and bake bread with the last of the flour and fill it with scraps of cheese and onion and herbs and eat steaming slices and hunks that fall apart while they laugh and sink onto her big iron bed, which has now been moved upstairs into the smaller of the two sitting rooms, and make love for hours on end without knowing who is who, if there is one gender or many, and for a brief moment forgets his fear of body and death, which is coming, it's coming, don't worry, it'll come, death comes in every story like this one, in the final cadence or maybe abruptly like a dumdum bullet forcing an entry in the midst of life and leaving it ripped apart, spread out across the earth.

Before that, however, the day arrives when the aunt, the mother's older sister, comes home from America. One afternoon when the girl and the young boy are visiting the maternal grandmother in her apartment in the nearest town, which isn't an actual town, just a collection of houses by the coast—a school, a supermarket, a set of traffic lights, and a tavern just inside the forest where young people meet on summer evenings to drink and dance and lie on the forest floor behind the tavern in the light from the open kitchen door and kiss and screw and brawl—the mother comes up the stairs with her older sister from America. Like every female member of an aristocratic family at a time when the aristocracy no longer exists but merely survives as impoverished remnants and is preserved solely in the physical posture, the gaze and, not least, in the supercilious mindset, the aunt also has a pet name, as does the mother, who is not called Benedikte, but Ditte, and the grandmother, who is not called Rigmor, but Pip, so the aunt in this story is not known by her name, Marianne, but is called Aunt Janne from America. Along with her older brother, the lawyer, who lives at the other end of the country, she is the head and final word in the family. But given that she lives in America and cannot exercise her authority on a daily basis, she has to do so far more effectively for the few days a year she is "at home in Denmark." The young boy, who is perhaps a girl, but does not yet know it, has so far only heard about the aunt, who lives in the state of Massachusetts on the east coast of America with her American husband, a professor of philosophy at the famous university MIT. They met in Rome, where she was on her Grand Tour and he was the youngest priest in Vatican City State and already picked out to be one of those cardinals who might at some point become Pope, but from the second he sees her, and she sees him see her, it's too late, before the week is out he has renounced his vocational vows and abandoned the monastery cell and Vatican City State and has even left the Catholic Church in order to devote his life to love and this young woman who is now Aunt Janne and at this very moment steps through the door from the entrance hall into the little room in the grandmother's apartment on the second floor in a humdrum block in the provincial town of Bogense, where he, the young boy, sits furthest away on the sofa and waits in inquisitive horror. She is tall and slim like her younger sister, but darker and utterly devoid of the inscrutability and the light that makes it impossible for the young boy ever to be finished with looking at the mother, because as soon as he glances away for a moment he has a feeling that he has not yet seen her. On the other hand, she, big sister Aunt Janne, emanates a daunting authority. She strides straight across the room toward him, but instead of getting up like a well-mannered boy he stays sitting, frozen, and she comes to a halt on the other side of the coffee table and looks down at him and reaches out her hand, and now at last he stands up, unfolds himself like a switchblade from his crevice in the sofa, and offers her his hand and says his name. What more? says the woman. What? he says, confused. What more are you called, your surname? He says his surname and her face shows no reaction, but she asks him where he was born and when, and his parents, what do they do and where do they live, has he got brothers and sisters, and what do they do, and what about him, what is he studying and if he hasn't yet embarked on a course of study, upon which course of study has he thought to embark, and at which university and when? And he tries all confused to answer these questions, stuttering, speechless really, he's still standing at attention, she hasn't yet signaled that he can sit down, she too is still standing at attention, but in a completely different way to him, not rigid with fear, but erect with patrician obligation and radiant destiny. He is rigid with self-consciousness and mortification, and at the same time laughter is bubbling up in him, I can't believe this, he thinks, brimming with happiness and shame and invulnerability, and later, far into the night, when the aunt has long since gone to bed in the guest room on the second floor in the white farmhouse, and even the mother has retired with her books in the four-poster bed by the window in the east-facing bedroom, and he is lying downstairs alongside the daughter, the niece, in her big iron bed in the girl's bedroom full of lace and pink and posters and an awful mess, and he is still dizzy, as if terminally exhausted and at the same time sleeplessly exalted, the girl at his side will laugh at him, laugh at his hopeless ordinariness, he who comes from just another ordinary family, one that undoubtedly has more money than hers, which in actual fact doesn't have any money at all, just effortlessly pretends to, but on the other hand his family doesn't have any history. He has been put to his life's test and he hasn't passed, and from now on the aunt from America will do everything in her power, not out of malice and not for any personal reasons whatsoever, purely from patrician obligation, to get him out of the story. But this entire story within the story, the story about Aunt Janne from America and her

American professor of philosophy, Uncle Bob, who had
been chosen to be one of Rome's forthcoming cardinals
and member of a future conclave, but who, from the moment he saw the young woman who would later become
Aunt Janne, had lost his faith, or rather had only then
begun to believe and understand that he had hitherto
been an unbeliever, and that the true god isn't the Catholic God, but is Love, all this improbable but entirely
credible love story is, like every story in this story, a
story in itself, which must constantly be interrupted and
then resumed until every story has reached its more or
less tragic ending.

But while everything is still possible, we need to see
all the characters because there are already several and
several more will turn up en route, main characters and
secondary characters and above all the other young boy,
who is actually the first and was here long before the
slim, oh so sensitive one entered, handsome Lars, the
girl's best friend and confidant, he looks like the slender one, they could be brothers and, just like brothers,
opposites: the delicate and vulnerable one and opposite
him a fit and robust Lars, the model young man, tall
and fair, an athletic body and beautiful hands with
long fingers that look as if they could do everything,
play tennis and basketball and piano and effortlessly
grasp and hold destiny, the radiant future, as if it were
not a gift but the most natural thing, voilà! He is every

mother-in-law's dream and undoubtedly also Aunt Janne from America's, if, that is, she hasn't already rumbled him and seen that he suffers from the same disastrous laziness as the niece, but without her ability to enjoy it, on the contrary, like any other gift he must let it slip from his hands, indolently and with a sigh let it be lost, and he, who looks as if he is the healthy one of the two young boys, the one who holds the future in his hands, will be the first to let go of it all and die, but not as in a melodrama, not in a reckless chase through the forest or the suburban residential neighborhoods, but slowly yield to the sweet despair which is sickness unto death. But to begin with, all the way through the endless summer, he just has to be there as a matter of course, Danish Lars, coming and going as he chooses, sitting up against the south-facing wall in the yard with his bare beautiful feet on the warm cobblestones and his face turned to the sun, all unthinking and empty-handed and not getting up until someone calls, and even then he remains seated and several minutes pass by and half hours before he finally turns up, sitting down at the table with a sigh and looking at the chaotic feast conjured up from yesterday's leftovers thinned down with a drop of fresh milk or some leeks from the neighbor's field, and without ever doing anything other than just sitting there and eating and chatting and laughing his charming and sigh-like laughter and occasionally getting up and wandering around a bit with dangling arms and those beautiful hands that never seem to catch hold of anything, not a book or a tool or another human being, but just like him pretend to be, étant donné, the incarnation of the future that will never come and where everything that is a possibility will finally become a reality. However, in the "for the time being" in which the story and life take place, he's just going to be allowed to stay there as a friend of the family, the third, prodigal son whose disastrous indolence has undoubtedly been rumbled by the aunt from America, but whom the mother with her supreme and all-forgiving grace just carries on loving with the same unreasonable love shown by the father to his returned son in Jesus's parable, and about whom the daughter is alone in occasionally being a little irritated without understanding that he isn't just lazy like she is, but that his idleness is fatal because in reality it is indolence itself, he can't face anything, not a thing, not even life, it's simply too much bother.

And if the story so far sounds like a dream, a glossy tale of the kind one occasionally—on holiday or a long-haul flight—allows oneself to lean back into and, as if it were sinful, a praline, vanish within for a brief moment, then it's because life is a dream, a dream from which you never wake up, but which one day is nonetheless suddenly long since over, but you're still here and can either use "the rest of your days" to forget and "get on with it" or on the other hand, like me, abandon what is and try to retrieve what was, even the tiniest little thing that has been lost, even what perhaps didn't really exist but nonetheless belongs in the story, call it forth and tell it so it doesn't vanish but on the contrary now at last becomes real and in a way more real than anything else.

But even in the dream, some things are just a dream, "the endless summer" for example, maybe it will never begin, maybe it's just the liberation of which the slender boy dreams, lying there in the damp basement room alongside the sleeping girlfriend and unable to fall asleep because of the unbearable lightness reigning in the farm, the same metallic soughing of completely real un-reality that underlies David Lynch's films, the girl at his side, sleeping her pleasure-filled sleep having just told him another of the stories that, until he met her, he had always thought were make-believe, and of which she with her just sixteen years already has so many that she apparently can't even keep them under control, they just sort of rise like bubbles out of her in the darkness as midnight approaches, lying there in the iron bed in her girl's room surrounded by the pink and pop posters of innocence, while he, who is already several years older, doesn't have any stories and never will have any other than the ones he creates himself, the darkness, and in the darkness her steady breathing, and upstairs the empty rooms he's walked through now and then without ever meeting another human being, and above them the second floor with the bedroom behind the closed door he has never dared open and where she must be lying now, because where else would she lie, the mother alongside this man with whom she must once have fallen in love and married and had two boys, a thought so absurd that he still can't quite believe it, how she, who emanates such a natural and sovereign inherent freedom, a superhuman and in fact inhuman deadly freedom that no other person would ever be able to tame, but would simply perish in the attempt to contain, how she could have fallen in love with this man who is not even, at least no longer, a man but more like a stick of dry wood, a splinter snapped off a sheet of chipboard, impossible to picture as anything other than a shadow in the periphery of the field of vision, because she must have done so, fallen in love with him, she hasn't taken him for the money's sake, she'd never do that, and anyway she must have met him while he was still just a trainee or assistant in an insignificant provincial bank and several years before he suddenly inherited from his father and from one day to the next quit his job and, rather than doing the same as his older brother Buller and investing his half of the inheritance in thoroughbred horses and securities, bought the estate that he, in reality, even with his sizeable inheritance, couldn't afford. The girl has just—in the darkness before she let herself slide down into her pleasure-filled sleep, in the already dreamy state where the seasons swap places and autumn is followed by yet another autumn—told him about the time they spent at the manor, a life that in reality only lasted eighteen months, from the day her stepfather without warning moved them from the small detached house on the out- skirts of a provincial town on the main Danish island of Sealand to the magnificent manor house in the east of Jutland, which he in fact could not afford and which he then, as landed proprietor, proved he didn't have the slightest notion how to run but started, from day one, to go bust, and without actually doing anything, on the contrary by *not* doing everything that needed to be done and that should be done every day in order to run an estate, had taken just those eighteen months to transform from a pipe dream into a bankruptcy. To begin with he had hired a handful of men to help him run the estate, men he had taken over from the former owner along with the fields, forests, and estate buildings, and who knew how things should be done, but after just a few months he was forced to lay them off and after that he had to deal with everything by himself, but instead of trying to do at least something he just wandered around the vast buildings, the barn and the machinery storage outhouse, the shut-down dairy and the cowsheds—which under the previous owner, who had closed down the entire side of operations dealing with livestock and con- centrated exclusively on the considerable acreage of fields suitable for crops, had been left empty—and then out across the fields like a proper squire inspecting his estate, but without issuing any orders because there was no longer anyone to carry out any orders, there were just fields, which at some point would have to be harvested, but by whom he had no idea so he just inspected the decline instead, until one day in late summer he got into his car and drove to the nearby provincial town and used the money that should or at least could have been spent on the imminent heating-up of the main building, with all its halls and rooms and a total of sixteen bathrooms and toilets, to buy a suitable arsenal of guns and from then on disappear with his gundog into the estate forest, not returning home until after dark and without ever bringing any quarry to speak of, no stag, not even a couple of gray geese, and without a word to anyone just sit down in his place at the head of the far too big dining table in the, for a family of two adults and three children and with neither aunts nor grandparents nor servants, far too big and now, with autumn gradually setting in, every day steadily colder dining room, in which he insisted they, being the landowning family they were, of course should have their evening meal, and ate what the mother put in front of him and which more often than not simply consisted of potatoes and the warmed-up leftovers of the pheasant or partridge he had brought home several days previously as his only quarry, without showing any sign of despair or panic and without suddenly shouting or hitting the bottle, on the contrary, he maintained a dogged and grim and puritanical discipline, rose with the sun every morning, drank a cup of coffee and ate a slice of bread with cheese while standing at the kitchen table wearing his purpose-bought hunting outfit and thereafter disappeared into the forest with his gun-dog. The two little brothers were still too young to go to school, but he had enrolled his stepdaughter, as is meet and proper for the daughter of a landed proprietor, at the only private school in the nearby provincial town and now every morning she took the bus and received tuition along with the town's other specially privileged children, who unlike her were not the children of landed propri-etors but simply the sons and daughters of the town's upper-middle class of doctors and dentists, lawyers and bank managers and sales directors and lived in quite ordinary, but of course rather spacious, detached houses and a few villas on the outskirts of town with lawns leading down to the many lakes and streams in the area, and who came to school every day wearing up-to-the-minute fashions bought from the fanciest boutiques in the shopping precinct or perhaps even all the way over in the heart of the provincial capital, and every day opened a colorful plastic lunchbox filled with slices of dark sourdough rye bread and white bread with interest-ing toppings, roast beef with rémoulade sauce and crispy fried onions, liver pâté with a slice of salt beef and aspic with raw onion rings and cress, pork tenderloin with scrambled egg and cress, home-made pâté with cucum-ber slices, and ate just what they fancied along with a

fizzy drink or a chocolate milk bought in the school
canteen, whereas every day she just had the same dented
tin box that her mother before her had used, with the
daily two half-rounds of rye bread spread with marga-
rine and topped with pre-sliced cold meats from the
cheapest supermarket in town, and rather than up-to-
the-minute fashions she went to school every morning
wearing her mother's cast-off trousers and sweaters and
throughout the entire autumn and winter the same pair
of green rubber boots, as if she didn't come from a
manor house but one of those smallholdings dotted all
over the place in the voids between provincial towns,
surrounded by an overgrown garden full of rusty junk
cars and old trailers on punctured sunken tires. Neither
her stepfather nor her mother had made any attempt
whatsoever to make contact with or be admitted to the
grander society of landowners and farmers in the neighborhood, they kept to themselves, barely spoke with the
neighbors, but, unlike the stepfather in his first-class
hunting outfit, the mother made no effort to look like a
landowner's wife, she just was one, innately, no matter
where you saw her, walking across the courtyard from
the main building to the stable or on horseback riding
along one of the many tracks or narrow gravel roads, she
emanated the effortless superiority and dignity that is
the exclusive prerogative of a landowner's wife from a
long lineage of landowners. She did what she wanted to,
and what she instinctively felt was her duty: she roused

her two young boys and dressed them and drove them to nursery and kindergarten and spent the rest of the day in the stable with her horse or riding along the surrounding tracks and forest trails, and mid-afternoon she unsaddled, groomed the horse, cleaned its hooves and gave it fresh water and hay, and then drove into town and picked up the two little boys and very occasionally also her daughter from school, drove them home, prepared some food for them, put the boys to bed, and sat for an hour or two in the kitchen with her daughter, drinking tea and chatting. One early-autumn evening at dinner in the as-of-yet not icy-cold but just a little uncomfortably chilly dining room, once she had put the dish of steaming potatoes, the bowl of vegetables, and the modest plate of undoubtedly pumped-up smoked saddle of pork on the table and sat down, she said, as if in passing, that next morning she was going to drive to the provincial capital, it was the start of the university semester. What are you going to do there? asked the stepfather. Study, she said and picked up her cutlery and cut a slice of pork and popped it into her mouth. You can't do that! he said. The mother did not respond. What are you going to study? he said. Art history and musicology, she said. That's ridiculous, he said, I cannot allow that. She did not respond to this either. You've got two little boys, he said. Resting her hands with knife and fork on the tabletop, she stared at him for a long time. Then she spoke his name. No more was said. They ate their food, and the mother and daughter cleared the table, did the washing up and put the two little boys to bed. And the next morning, having dropped the boys off at kindergarten and nursery, she drove all the way to the provincial capital.

Some days later, the stepfather had sold off the first piece of land, at an utterly ridiculous price, as she heard from the daughter on one of the neighboring farms with whom she some mornings took the bus into town where the neighbor's girl went to one of the ordinary state schools. The stepfather used the money from the sale to invest in a detective who, on the two days a week when the mother drove into the provincial capital in order to attend her courses at the university, discreetly and without any of her fellow students or lecturers or professors at the Faculty or the Institute for Interdisciplinary Aesthetic Studies ever noticing anything, tailed her and subsequently, twice a week, reported back to the stepfather and, moreover, listened in to each and every incoming and outgoing conversation on the estate telephone. Who told you that? asked the young boy. My mother, said the girl. And how did she know? She just knew, said the girl, my mother knows things like that, you can't hide anything from her. What's more, the stepfather had admitted as much, again at the dining table, one evening in late autumn, the mother had—again with absolute calm and without putting down her cutlery and without looking at him—said that the telephone in the house was being tapped, she could hear it, and moreover she was being tailed every time she went to town, she had noticed the same man several times, a perfectly run-of-the-mill man like you, she said and looked at him for a second, without anger, quite calmly, in front of a newsstand where he was pretending to examine a tabloid poster, and another time in the parking lot of the university campus, where he fumbled for a long time, far too long, she said and again looked at the stepfather and this time with a faint, almost compassionate or charitable smile, with the keys to his car. Yes, said the stepfather, it had proven necessary, he could no longer trust her. No more was said. They ate their dinner, and the mother and daughter rose from the table, cleared the dishes and washed up, and the mother put the two little brothers to bed, while the stepfather first remained seated, for what seemed like an eternity, in his place as master of the house at the head of the far too long dining table with his forearms resting on each side of the void left by the long-since cleared-away plate, and stared ahead as if he was trying, in his own self, to embody one of the painted portraits of the male heads of the family that should have bedecked the walls here in the dining room of the manor house, but of which there was not a single specimen for the simple reason that he was not the latest generation in a renowned lineage of Rosenkrantzs, Ahlefeldts, Billes, or Brahes, but just the son of an enterprising businessman in a mid-Sealand market town, a man without any kind of education who had worked his way up from the bottom and who had never had his portrait painted and had not even been photographed on his own but always in the bosom of his family with his wife and two sons or surrounded by business associates in front of a site or after a lunch at which an important collaboration agreement or deal had been reached, and afterward he eventually got up and walked through the hall and out onto the main staircase and stood in the gloomy dulling yellowish glow from the lamp above the door and smoked a cigarette, and then another one, and another, while the gundog sat at his side like a figure on a coat of arms. To begin with, every evening, when he came in after his day-long inspection of the estate buildings and fields, he had always changed for dinner, first out of his squire's outfit and later out of his hunting getup into a simpler and more comfortable evening ensemble—slacks, shirt, and shoes—but, after the brief exchange of words across the dining table about telephone tapping and "the tail," he no longer changed his clothes when he came indoors after the day's hunt, just put on a different pair of hunting boots, not yet used and still shop-window-shiny, which clicked discreetly on the old wooden floor when he stepped into the dining room, as if, in the state of emergency in which the family and estate found themselves, it had also, unfortunately, proven necessary to be in a state of preparedness, in full uniform and ready to launch into action whenever the special intelligence agency raised the alarm. But neither he nor the mother passed further comment on the state of alert or the brief exchange of words about telephone tapping and "the tail," and over the next many months nothing happened. They continued with their normal and peculiar lives; the girl went to school and spent time with her friends, who with the exception of one were not classmates from the private school but daughters from the surrounding smaller farms with whom she traveled every morning on the bus into town; the mother took care of the horses and the two small brothers and two or three times a week she drove into the provincial capital to attend her courses at the university; at the very last minute, without telling anyone, the stepfather had sold the entire harvest to one of the other landowners in the region, the girl at least hadn't heard a word about it, suddenly one morning a whole convoy of agricultural machinery came rolling in a slow thunder along the country road at the end of the long avenue of elms, then fanned out across the fields, combine harvesters as big as ferries sailing through the dry golden corn and raising a firmament of dust in their wake, and a good many smaller machines she didn't know the names of because she'd never lived in the countryside, not in Denmark at least, but had grown up, for the first six or nine years, with her grandparents in a little colony of northern Europeans in a mountain village on the Canary Islands, and later in a perfectly ordinary detached house in a residential neighborhood on the outskirts of a small town on the island of Sealand. On a couple of occasions she had seen the stepfather exchange a few words with one of the drivers or helmsmen at the edge of one of the fields, and just once a big jeep had pulled into the yard and a middle-aged man—who wasn't in "uniform" but was wearing a pair of high, dusty, and well-worn leather boots, some kind of breeches or plus fours, and a khaki shirt with the sleeves rolled up, but even so, and in an utterly more credible way than the stepfather, didn't just look like but *was* an authentic squire, a landowner—had gotten out and held a long conversation with the stepfather, at times leaning over a lot of documents and maps, probably of the estate, which he had spread out on the dusty hood of the jeep. Apart from that, the stepfather had behaved as if he had nothing whatsoever to do with either the harvest or the fields; early in the morning, he disappeared into the forests with his gundog, and it wasn't until after dark, once the combines, which often carried on long into the night, had switched on their work lights and now really did look like ferries or maybe more like tankers on their way across an endless and dark and completely calm sea, that he stepped in through the main entrance, changed into his "indoor boots" and sat down to dinner—alone, the mother and daughter and two little brothers had long since left the table—removed the lid from the serving dish and tureen and ate the cold leftovers. A few weeks later, the convoy of agricultural machinery rolled off below the low luminous September skies, leaving the fields perfectly harvested and, for a while at least, you might believe that the estate management was in the best of hands. And for the rest of the autumn and the early winter, the stepfather's conduct was actually what you would expect of a squire: he participated in the hunting season and did his duty in keeping game stocks on the estate hunting terrain and in the forests at an appropriate level. He behaved in a proper manner except that he never—as a genuine squire would have done—organized the shooting parties that would have been necessary for the management of wildlife; he always went out on his own, his only company being the faithful gundog, and he never returned with any large game, just a bunch of pheasants now and then, a brace of partridges, or a mallard. One evening in late February, he hadn't changed into his "indoor boots," but had walked into the dining room and sat down at the table wearing his dirty hunting boots. The elder of the two little brothers had run in and come to a halt, staring at the trail of dust and hardened mud from the doorstep to the seat at the head of the table, and said "wow, you dirty the floor, Daddy!" but neither the stepfather nor the mother had reacted, and the remainder of the evening meal had passed exactly as usual. When the mother and the daughter had risen to clear the table after the meal, the stepfather had asked them to leave the dishes where they were for the time being and go into the large sitting room instead as there was a matter he would like to talk over, a matter that concerned them all. The girl looked at her mother, and the mother lifted the smallest brother from the chair, took both boys by the hand and walked in front of the girl to the largest of the sitting rooms. They sat down on the big sofa, which raised a bit of dust, having been neither used nor brushed for months, and stared into the empty fireplace, in which a fire had not yet been lit during the time they had lived on the estate. After a couple of minutes the stepfather came in, still wearing his hunting outfit and the dirty hunting boots, but now also holding his best gun. He locked the door behind him and then also the door to the adjoining rooms, put the keys in his trouser pocket, stood in front of the fireplace and looked above their heads at the slightly paler patches on the wall where the former owner's many paintings had hung. It now appeared, he said, that he was right, he had not been able to trust the mother, her so-called studies at the university had not been the *real* reason she had started going into town several times a week, and that really went without saying because why did she suddenly want a university educa-tion, an utterly useless one into the bargain, that would never lead to a *real* job; the reason she had started going into town was that she had taken a lover. The mother didn't say a word, she looked at him, calmly, protractedly. Then she said his name. She looked down and almost imperceptibly shook her head and took the two little brothers' hands and placed them in her lap. For a long time it was quiet. Then the stepfather said that she didn't need to worry, he hadn't gone mad, it wasn't something he just sensed or "imagined." He had proof. Again she simply looked at him, protractedly, calmly, but without saying a word, not even his name. There was no hurry, he said, he had plenty of time, as far as he was concerned they could stay here for as long as necessary, the boys hadn't started school yet. What do you mean? she said. You know very well, he said, you just have to say it. What is it you want me to say? she said. Nothing in particular, he said, you just have to say it like it is. She uttered a little sound, a snort of air out through her nose, almost as if she was laughing, and shook her head and looked down. That I was right, he said, I couldn't trust you; as if you don't have enough, as if you want for anything, two little boys, a horse, and eight hundred eighty-six acres of land, and one more into the bargain, not even from an earlier marriage, but just the result of a drunken screw. That is enough! she burst out in a very clear voice, shrill as the shattering of crystal glass, and held her breath for a long time and exhaled again slowly, and again and in a very calm voice said his name, which now sounded less than ever like the name of a squire, but just like the name of a naughty boy or a wimp. It's up to you entirely, he said, I've got plenty of time. Could you not at least sit down, she said. I am a landowner, he said, and while that is so, I have a mind to walk and stand and sit exactly on and in my property whenever I choose. She nodded slowly and looked down and nodded again. What is it you want? she said quietly. Nothing, he said, you just have to say it like it is. I don't know what you're talking about, she said. The stepfather laughed, a curt, loud, hysterical laugh. Yes, she said, yes yes, of course I know what you're talking about. It just doesn't have anything to do with reality. She raised her head and looked at him for a long time. Then, for the third time, she spoke his name.

They had stayed there for the rest of the evening and throughout the night, in the sitting room in front of the empty and dark and cold fireplace. It wasn't long before first the younger and then the older of the two little brothers fell asleep, their heads on each of the mother's thighs. The girl had asked once if she could go to the toilet, and the stepfather had put the key in the door and opened it and said to the mother that now was the time if she wanted to go too, but the mother had just shaken her head, and he had locked the door behind them and gone with the stepdaughter to the nearest of the sixteen bathrooms and toilets and waited outside the door like an armed sentry or bouncer at a post-Soviet discotheque and had let her walk past him back toward the sitting-room door, which he had unlocked and let her through and then locked again behind them and put the key in his pocket. At no point during the night had he sat down,

now and then he walked back and forth in front of the
fireplace, again like a sentry, and late in the night he had
suddenly vanished into the adjoining room and returned
with the gun in one hand and the dish of cold and long-
since dried-up supper leftovers in the other, placing it
in front of them on the coffee table, but neither she nor
the mother touched the food; a couple of times the girl
had briefly dozed off and then woken up again, the second or third time it was beginning to get light and the
mother still hadn't said a word, not since her apparently
last and decisive word, the stepfather's name: Mads. Suddenly the normally perfectly behaved dog, which had
and knew its place out in the large scullery behind the
kitchen far away at the other end of the house, started
to howl. For a while they sat on the sofa listening to the
dog's peculiar and melancholy and disconsolate howling,
the younger of the two brothers woke up and rubbed
his eyes and said, what's that, Mom? The mother didn't
answer, just stroked his hair soothingly and looked at the
stepfather. He didn't say a word, just stood at attention
as he had done for most of the last twelve or fourteen
hours. Then he walked across to the door, purposefully,
like a soldier, unlocked it and went out, leaving it wide
open behind him, and vanished off to the other end of
the house. They remained seated in their places on the
sofa for a few minutes, listening to the dog's howling
turn into a chastened but delighted whimpering, then a
door slammed in the distance and a moment later they

saw the stepfather and the dog walk across the yard and out across the fields.

Properly speaking, what the stepfather had said was true, she was just the result of an arbitrary screw. Her mother—being the youngest of the three siblings, the afterthought, her father's "shining little angel"—had always been given everything she pointed at, and was allowed to do exactly what she wanted. Unlike her two older, disciplined and conscientious siblings, she didn't go straight from lower secondary school to upper secondary school, but at the age of just sixteen had moved in with her first boyfriend, Jesper, a tall and fair and shy young man who, like her, came from a good family. And one night after or perhaps even during a dorm party, when the boyfriend just didn't happen to be there, and she'd had a drop too much to drink, she had spent a long time chatting with an irresistible dark-complexioned and almost black-eyed Jewish guy, who it later turned out had been just fifteen years old (but apparently rather mature sexually), and had apparently also had it off with him. At any rate, she got pregnant, which at that time, when the pill had just been invented, wasn't only unfortunate, but also fairly idiotic when you were just sixteen years of age, and neither she nor her boyfriend had so much as started further education yet. But she didn't try to hide anything, she and the boyfriend loved one another, sooner or later they'd have a child anyway, so why not now when it had happened quite naturally (she had long since forgotten the little affair during the dorm party (and it really was little, the whole thing had lasted ten-fifteen minutes tops), at any rate she couldn't see why she should think anything of it, it was nothing, it was Jesper the boyfriend she loved, there had been no doubt at any point, and purely in terms of statistics it was impossible, it could only be Jesper), the entire family was immediately informed of the good news and was of course somewhat surprised, the two older siblings came home to the ritual Sunday lunch in the parents' house and had already taken the necessary decision, the elder sister gave her little sister a shrill telling-off, while the older brother, who was the eldest and read law at the University of Copenhagen, waited calmly for the right moment, whereupon he pronounced judgment: there was nothing to discuss, a termination must be arranged, of course, and as swiftly as possible. The mother wept and the father, sitting in his place in the big leather chair by the window, looked his daughter in the eye and nodded in a fatherly fashion. She idolized her father, and equally her older brother, she put them above every other living soul, including the boyfriend and every one of the boyfriends and husbands she would later have, throughout her life she always listened, and with the deepest gravity, to the advice and decisions her older brother had and had taken regarding her future, and always did everything she could to follow them. Also now, of course, she accepted his decision. She just couldn't act on it. She was going to have a baby. The boyfriend had also been present throughout the entire session, he was standing right behind her and didn't say a word. He was terrified and proud. When the beech trees came into leaf, she gave birth to a lovely little daughter, and a few months later she started at upper secondary level evening school. On weekdays the girl was looked after at her maternal grandparents' home, she quickly became accustomed to being bottle-fed, and very soon she was more or less living with her grandparents and just occasionally visiting her mother and the boyfriend in their student dorm room, which was not really purpose-made for a child. For the first year babies just look like babies, but after a year or so the grandmother told her husband that it seemed for all the world as if the girl's eyes were going to be brown; could you have brown eyes if both your parents were blue-eyed? The father summoned the daughter home and had a one-on-one conversation with her, blue eyes staring into blue eyes, and the daughter said that there had never been anything else at all, just the once and it had meant absolutely nothing, to her there was only one who was the father and that was the one she loved. The father was nonetheless of the opinion that she ought to have a chat with her boyfriend and, as always and as far as was humanly possible, she followed her father's advice. That very evening she told her Jesper that he might not be the girl's father, but he refused to

listen, he had difficulty breathing, his eyes shone mani-
cally and he hissed that this was totally insane, she must
have mommy brain, from not breast-feeding, that she
was perverted, it was his child, she was exactly like he
had been, both his mother and his father said so, he
could feel it, she was his daughter and he would never
let any other man come between them, over his dead
body. Later on, the father also tried to speak to his son-
in-law, in confidence, but nothing could be done. As the
years passed, it became increasingly apparent that the
girl bore no likeness whatsoever to her father, or to her
mother come to that; she wasn't slim and fair and spikey,
but round and soft and brown-eyed. It was obvious to
everyone, apart from the man who saw himself as her
father, and then of course the girl, who was still too
young to be able to see herself as anything other than a
foregone conclusion. When she was three years old, the
grandfather sold the elegant and renowned seaside hotel
in the north of Sealand, which he and his wife had run
in recent years, and they moved to a small mountain
village high up in the Canary Islands, and the girl went
with them, started at the local village school, spoke
Spanish with her Spanish girlfriends and looked exactly
like a little Spanish lass, one of the dark-complexioned
ones with Moorish ancestors and almost black-brown
eyes. Her tall, fair-haired and blue-eyed parents visited
a couple of times a year, and she proudly showed them
off to her Spanish girlfriends, who thought they looked

like something from a fairytale, fairies or angels. They had met when both were very young, and as they approached twenty they started growing apart, or rather, she grew apart from him (as she later said: I'm actually very old-fashioned, I'm faithful to my husbands, each and every one, for seven years on end. But what about me? the girl shouted. Stina! said the mother, you are of course an exception! And then she laughed, and as always the girl was outraged), she met someone else and they moved in together, and from then on the two fairies or angels visited separately, but they were still just as much her parents. After six years spent as a little Spanish girl in a Spanish school, who like all her Spanish girl-friends and their siblings and parents and grandparents prayed to God and wept loudly and inconsolably and for days on end when the great Generalissimo Franco died, her mother, who had in the meantime married a dogged young man with a small, fair mustache and the good Nordic name Mads, son of an enterprising businessman from mid-Sealand, and had moved with him to a small detached house on the outskirts of the town where he worked as an up-and-coming clerk in the local bank, and was expecting his (yes, his, this time there was no doubt (either)) child, decided to bring her daughter home from the Canary Islands so she could grow up alongside her little sister or brother and attend a Danish school and become a Danish girl. The little Spanish girl with the colorful Catholic scheme of things was put in one of the utterly ordinary Danish provincial elementary schools, which at that time were still ethnically pure and without so much as a hint of anything worryingly foreign, and now she didn't look like her parents or her girlfriends and their parents, but something quite different, something both thrilling and exotic, but also always different, and, like every other child, in the early years she too just had to live with the fact that that's how it was and how she was. But deep down, in the Catholic scheme of things she had brought along from the village in the Canary Islands, the true story gradually took shape: she had, of course, been adopted, her parents or grandparents had of course found her among other foundlings at a children's home down in Las Palmas and had initially tried to take her directly to Denmark, but that had proven to be disastrous, she had wasted away in the cold and dark alien north, and as she lay on her deathbed the grandfather, being the Danish hero and Viking he was, had taken the most vital decision of his life, in great haste he had sold his beloved seaside hotel and with his wife and the young dying princess he had moved to the Canary Islands, high up in the mountains, far from the town with its noise and pollution (a word with which she first became acquainted when she was again taken to Denmark and "detained" in the Danish elementary school class where it was one of the buzz words of the day, the girls and boys having heard their parents and Danish teacher use it, and they in turn had heard it on the

television news), in the clear mountain air into which she
had been born some time ago and which was now her
only hope. One afternoon, when she had just turned
twelve years of age and was for once alone with her
mother in the kitchen while the boys were either out in
the garden or were momentarily playing relatively ami-
cably in their room, she took a deep breath and spoke
The Truth: Mom, I know that Jesper isn't my real father
and that you aren't my real mother, you just adopted me!
The mother turned from the cutting board on which she
was chopping onions for the meatballs and gazed at her
for a long time. And then she said that wasn't true, she
really was her real mother, but it was correct that Jesper
wasn't her biological father, he was called Jacob. All was
silent for a moment, neither the mother nor the daughter
knew what to say, they just stared at one another. Then
the mother walked past her and out into the entrance
hall, put down the knife, picked up the telephone and
dialed a number and spoke for a long time, first with the
one then with the other, then a third and possibly a
fourth and fifth and sixth before she eventually hung up
and came back into the kitchen and said that actually she
had thought it would be impossible, like finding a needle
in a haystack, she said, but now she had succeeded, she
had got hold of someone who knew him and who had
given her his number, and, yes, she had in fact just spoken with him, he lived all the way over in southern Jutland now, but tomorrow he would drive over to them in

Sealand to see her. No-o! the girl screamed, nothing else, just "no-o!" she wept uncontrollably and hysterically and threw herself onto the floor and got up and ran into her room and ripped all the pop posters off the walls and dived onto the bed with her head at the wrong end and burrowed her face into the duvet and screamed and hoped she would be suffocated. By the time stepfather Mads arrived home from the bank, she had calmed down a little, but she was still lying on the bed, and the mother told the stepfather that the daughter was ill and had a fever and unfortunately she probably wouldn't be well enough to go to school next day, and the stepfather said she'd have to sort that out herself, he walked past the door to her room without looking in and flopped down in the corner sofa in the sitting room and switched on the television, and the mother followed with his coffee. All night long the girl lay awake imagining her truly real and far-fetched and apparently also "biological" father, tall and muscular and Spanish Jewish, a bit like a gypsy chieftain, one of those who occasionally turned up at the village in the mountains with his harem of dancing and singing women and girls of her own age with bare dirty feet and little bells around their ankles, and who wore big chunky rings of gold not just on the ring finger like grandfather, but on all eight or nine remaining digits. Next morning, after the stepfather had left for the bank, she got up and dressed, not in a gypsy princess outfit, but like a perfectly ordinary Danish girl in her most

recently purchased clothes, from the cheapest of the
three boutiques on the main street, and sat down to wait
on the chair by the telephone in the entrance hall. At one
thirty—one-and-a-half hours after the appointed time,
and after she had long since become hysterical and had
shouted at her mother that it was all a lie, that it was just
something she, the mother, had made up, and that any
idiot and even the boys in her class could see she was
adopted—a large, round and soft and dark-skinned and
almost completely black-haired already-balding young
man, the sun making the top of his head shine, walked
up the driveway and stepped onto the doorstep and rang
the bell. Mom! she whispered, what shall I do! Open the
door, of course, her mother said calmly from the kitchen.
I can't! she whispered. And then she opened the door.
The father, who had just turned twenty-eight and—apart
from that one time eleven years earlier, when he had
been sixteen and more or less lived or at least hung out
in the recently liberated Freetown Christiania military
base, and where a beautiful slim fair-haired young hippie
he vaguely remembered having seen once before somewhere or other, maybe during a Steppenwolf concert, had
emerged from the hash haze and walked toward him
with a straw basket on her arm, and had carefully lifted
a scarf from the basket and said, look, your daughter!,
not that he had been able to see anything, he was too
stoned, it was too fuzzy, the light from the stage flick-
ered, and the basket was dark, or catch what the young

woman had said, for that matter, or hear it as anything other than just one of those things you said, like "love" and "peace" and "if we think really hard, maybe we can stop this rain"—had never seen his daughter and had in fact forgotten or never really grasped that he even had a daughter, and therefore, despite his "artistic" temperament, couldn't picture the yesterday so-abruptly-announced twelve-year-old daughter as anything other than a sweet little girl, he simply didn't look at the almost full-grown girl with large soft breasts who opened the door, he stared with nervous curiosity past her shoulder, looking out for the real little girl, his daughter, who had to be in there somewhere behind the step-sister or paternal aunt or nanny (or whatever she was) who had answered the door when he rang the bell. It's me! she said in a very small voice, overcome and forlorn, and then he saw her. It was like standing face to face with his missing sister, the closest he had ever been to seeing himself in someone else. But he couldn't believe that this young woman in front of him was meant to be his daughter, and maybe he never took it in for real during the few years they were to know one another. And what is your name? he said. Christina, she said, or just Stina. Stina, he said. And neither of them said anything else. A minute passed, and then the mother came out and said his name and invited him in for a cup of coffee. They sat in the kitchen for an hour, and the mother chattered on in her clear and vigorously vivacious and urbane voice, while the father just sat there like a big, heavy and melancholy boy grasping the coffee cup in his lap with both hands, and nodded and glanced evasively from the one of these two total strangers to the other, from the tall upright fair woman to the round, soft, brown-eyed young woman, from the mother and to the daughter, who just stared at him. Well, he eventually said, I should probably be on my way now. After some years spent in the hash hazes and various communes in the vicinity of Copenhagen, he had got together with a handful of people his own age who wanted to do something, create a completely new world of love and community and solidarity, and given that the revolution, which was of course the only option, was also somewhat abstract and hard to get going, they started by setting up a group theater, one of the "floating islands" where life and art, work and leisure, revolution and reproduction, formed a synthesis, which was a sign of the times, and they moved back to nature, all the way over to Jutland, where hardly any of them had ever set foot before, and rented a dilapidated mansion or an abandoned mill on the outskirts of a smallish town and lived together in a little communal Utopia, where life and art and work and leisure, production and consumption formed a synthesis, and no one had his or her own room, own lover, or own underpants, even the pill and tampons and concomitant menstruation were just as much the men's responsibility and property as the women's. At first, the local community, which consisted mainly of native-born southern Jutlanders, was skeptical of this sudden invasion of Copenhagen hippies with their unrelenting clowning and Chinese propaganda and opium plants in the *front* yard, but on the other hand the State, even back then, and unlike the State in the larger European countries, was above all disposed to listen to what its citizens had to say, and to accommodate their wishes and their new ways of living, so within a couple of years their little Utopia had already been granted the status of regional theater with municipal funding, annual budgets and accounts, and the obligation to tour through-out the district. And while the old reactionary world (order) thus proved to be more than commodious in also embracing its own opposite, revolution and the new world, in the long run it turned out that life in the little new world was more than utopian enough. The synthesis of life and art, work and leisure, individual and com-munity, was in reality extremely claustrophobic, most of the members were swiftly possessed of an initially secret and mortifying longing to take time off now and then, not so much from working with the theater, which most of them still found fun, but chiefly from one another. Instead of a grand cosmic love, they got together two and two in small, indeed progressive but ultimately quite ordinary petit-bourgeois couples, and moved into one of the small row- or standard-houses that the State and its municipal authorities with exemplary provident timing allowed to sprout up around every town during this very period. In his case, it had turned out that the longing to take time off from one another now and then was not—unlike the outlook of the others—just a desire to separate work and leisure and have a bit of private life. The languor, which in the girl most people ultimately saw as being a provocative, unproductive pleasure-indulgence, was in him primarily a completely personal dromedary tempo. He wasn't lazy, he could actually get things done, but that required him being allowed to work in rhythm with his own breath, which was by no means the tempo of the commune. Actually he preferred to be himself, not just in the new private life with his girlfriend, but also in the stage work making little plays for children aged six to twelve, now the last patch of Utopia where the group's shows about another world still took place. To begin with, as an exception, he was allowed to do his own one-man shows, which the others in the group had to approve before he was given the okay to perform them for the rest of the old society, but after some years he opted completely out of the group and formed his own one-man theater, which wasn't called the Theater of Cruelty or The Poor Theater, Chariot of the Sun, Odin or The Mill, but was just called by his name, the one he was and not anyone or anything else. As it happened, this very evening he was due to give a guest performance at a little theater in Copenhagen, which was why he'd had time almost without any prior notice to pop in and see the daughter he had no idea about, or had at least long since forgotten he had. He stood up and the mother, still chattering on euphorically about all the memories this reunion had suddenly brought flooding back, also stood up, and only the girl, who hadn't said a word during the moment or half or whole hour the visit had lasted, remained seated. Stina! the mother said with a laugh, and so she got up, and father and daughter stood face to face, round and mild and soft and equally impotent, while the mother at their side laughed and said they resembled one another like two drops of heavy water. The half-bald young man suddenly opened his large arms and put them around her in a warm and sort of rocking embrace, not like a father, but something bigger, a big old animal, a bear maybe, something immensely safe and oceanic and far too overwhelming. He was about to say something, her name, "my all-grown-up girl," just something, but he didn't say a word. He let go of her and walked out of the door and down the driveway and a little way along the road, where the old van was parked, containing his one-man show about a different and better world where adults are just big children and life is a dream, got in and drove off. Over the next couple of years she visited him and his girlfriend a few times in their row-house on the outskirts of the little town in southern Jutland, and once in a blue moon, when he was doing a guest performance in Copenhagen, he might pop in for a cup of coffee during the afternoon while the stepfather was still at work in the bank. Just six months after the first visit, he and his girlfriend had a baby, and two years later they had one more. She called them "my little brother and little sister," they didn't look like her, they mostly took after their mother, small, delicate and fair, but when she visited them she saw how they quite instinctively crawled around his bulky frame and with their little feet sank into his soft stomach as if they were one flesh, one big and warm and alive and multi-armed body. She could see that he looked like her more than anyone else in the whole world, and every time they were together she made sure she was standing or sitting within his field of vision in the hope that he would (finally) catch sight of his daughter. But he continued to look at her as if she was just another grown-up girl, and he treated her like he treated everyone else: steadily and genially and patiently. She yearned for him to tell her off, be totally unreasonable and let fly at her like a proper father, and at times she was overcome by the intense anger and feeling of abandonment that is typical of a daughter, but none of it helped. Perhaps it had something to do with his very particular tempo, the sea-sluggish slowness they shared, perhaps he needed time, several years, maybe more, before eventually, one day, he would understand that he was her father. But within a few years it turned out that the self-same indolence he had passed on to her didn't merely apply to his external organs—the soft face, the long swaying arms, the hefty, slightly drooping belly that spread in a soft belt right round to his back and overhung his waist and far too narrow hips—but also to his inner organs: some years after she and the two little ones had entered his world, the one kidney took a rest, was treated at the hospital, where they tried to get it working again, but after a year or so things looked doubtful and so a new one was ordered, and while he wandered around waiting for the new, third kidney, the second one failed; and many years later when the whole story and certainly "the endless summer" had definitely come to an end, and the delicate, slender young boy had fallen back into the other and far too ordinary world and had himself become a kind of actor, who made his own little solo shows and was giving guest performances in the provincial capital, a small and quite unremarkable woman he seemed to recall from another time in another world approached him and introduced herself as the theater administrator and asked if he recognized her. Yes, he said, yes yes, and plainly had no idea who she was. I'm Laust's and Gedske's mother, she said, Jacob's partner. And Jacob? he said. For a moment, endless and beyond any timescale, she simply looked at him, in deep surprise and utterly adrift. Then she took his hand. Jacob, she said, but he's dead.

The very next morning after Jacob's first visit, the girl's mother had rung the man who had hitherto called himself and been her father and said that she had been obliged to tell her the truth. What truth? he said in a thin quivering voice (and was already about to weep), *your* truth?! he yelled. Jesper, she said. But he wouldn't listen, not even to his own name would he listen, certainly not that. He wept and yelled and whispered that she was a whore, that you couldn't trust other people, that he was all alone in the world. She asked if he wanted to talk to the girl, but he didn't. The girl never saw him again. For the twelve years she had been in the world, she had loved this tall, fair, rather nervy young man as her own father, she had been thrilled to sleeplessness every time he was to visit the village up in the mountains and she was to parade him in front of her Spanish girlfriends, first as an elf prince and later a genuine Viking, and later she had felt like a real teenager when he took her on little holidays to Greek islands or Paris, he had gone on being her father even after she had realized that she was adopted, she loved him, and now all of a sudden he wouldn't see her. What have I done? she wept. It has nothing to do with you, her mother said. Then who is it to do with? It's all just about him, Stina. Then he's never loved me? Yes, said the mother, of course he has, and that's why he won't see you. I don't understand, said the girl. No, said the mother, people are like that. Then I don't want to be like people! said the girl. But she soon forgot about that, just like she forgot about all sorts of other things, appointments, the time, that all of a sudden it was already Monday and she had to go to school, she never forgave anyone for anything, the pain and sorrow just took cover in the here and now, which for her was not one moment but a flow into the boundless world by which she was absorbed and inhabited and with which she formed and was a synthesis, just like she was also her wickedly messy bedroom and her presence in "the endless summer" at the farmhouse, as if that was it, and the future would never arrive, a feature most people who met her found charming and enviable and a feature "we could all really learn from," whereupon they returned to the world and time and all the things that had to be accomplished, and got themselves educations and partners and children and first a supply job and later a permanent job, which after a few years they left in favor of a different and more challenging job and a different and more dynamic partner, something and someone to keep them in motion and carry them forward and perhaps many years later they might meet her again quite by chance on the street and see that she is still exactly the same, someone who time and then the future have passed by, so the luxuriance they had found seductive twenty years ago is now just blurry and shapeless, not luxuriant, but shamelessly (or helplessly) overweight, just like the life in the still dancing eyes, which makes them shudder and look at their cell phones and say how nice to see you and we'll have to get together one of these days, I've really got to be going, bye for now! and turn their back on her and vanish around the corner with the frisson of shame and relief that remains when, for a brief moment, you have come face to face with self-delusion and become aware that it is the worst, far worse than your own treachery.

That evening, yes, now we're embedded back in the very evening that is both the beginning of the story, or at least the opening through which he falls out of the world and into what is going to be "the endless summer," and the moment before the story begins, and he is as yet far from the weird cobweb-flighty female being he will one day become, but is still just "this fetching young boy with the delicate features and the big eyes": in ten minutes they will be going onstage—as mentioned, it is only their first or second gig—instruments and gear are waiting in the colored light on the dais in the school canteen, which for several hours has been full of totally unfamiliar senior-high students who have built up their courage and a degree of recklessness with a drink or two before coming here and have built it up even more during the meal and have now reached something like a state of near hysteria, the four or five other members of the band, the drummer, bass and keyboard players, singer, and the other guitarist are standing next to the stage or in the classroom they have been allocated as their band room with the obligatory two crates of, respectively, beer and mixed soft-drinks, discussing effects pedals with an admiring, pimpled sophomore student, or flirting with those girls who will always, no matter how unkempt a rock musician might look, hang around by the door to the band room. No matter what, he's too shy and incapable of playacting, so he's drifted a little away from everything, out into the entrance hall and down a staircase to the basement and cloakroom where seven hundred winter coats and hats and scarves and gloves and muddy boots from farms and small towns across the entire northern part of the island hang squashed tightly together or are just dumped in piles on the synthetic grayish-blue carpet, smelling sour from the sleet and nauseously sweet from deodorant and cheap perfume. All of a sudden, a girl comes whirling down the staircase, not elegantly or self-assured, but breathlessly cavorting in a flapping of coat and scarves and bristling fingers, good heavens! she says and smiles at him and goes on talking as if it's the most natural thing in the world, as if she's known him forever, time suddenly ran away with me, she gasps and laughs, turning scarlet, not from shame, just from life, and he asks her so when should she have been here? Six o'clock, she gasps, for the potluck dinner, of course! But it's nearly nine o'clock, he says. Good heavens! she says and laughs and throws her coat on top of five others and runs to the mirror and sputters and chatters away while she gives everything a bit of a tweak. He just stands watching her. He doesn't know if she's beautiful, she's just so overwhelmingly alive, all this blushing and chattering and gasping for breath, the arms and fingers flitting all over the place, and suddenly she's gone. He walks up the stairs, through the crowd of teenagers, back to the stage, and the others ask where the hell he's been. Down in the cloakroom, he says, to the toilet. Later in the evening, when the concert is over, or at least once they've stopped playing and have left the stage—no one was dancing anyway, and even the heavily-painted girls, the groupies, who had flirted with the others in the doorway to the band room before they went on, have been shouting if they couldn't "play somethin' we know!" and some of the boys, the bumpkins, haven't only thrown tomatoes and eggs, but also melting butter and long foil trays full of liver pâté onto the stage (which gradually started to stink like a sweaty dunghill), and suddenly there was a power cut—he again drifts away from the others, but not down into the basement this time, on the contrary straight into the worst of the tumult, where intoxication has long been reckless and mindless, and apparently no one notices him any longer, he is free and gets all the way up to the bar before he's surrounded by a bunch of big country lads with disco mullets who jab their beer bottles in his chest and sway right into his face shouting "why the hell don't y'all just scram, get lost, no-damn-one asked ya t'come here an' rooin our party, ya can't even play!' and suddenly she pops up, laughing, between them and puts her arms around the necks of the two biggest and kisses them on the cheek and tells him not to listen to them, they're okay guys, they're just a bit drunk, and later still, after they've loaded up the car and the others are sitting in the back of the truck with the extra crate of beers just waiting for him, standing there in the snowstorm smiling and nodding to her and her girlfriend who are both chatting at the same time, the second guitarist suddenly jumps down from the truck and tells the two girls to just come along into town, and later in the morning, once they have ended up at the last and worst bar, where there are frequent shootings, that's what it's like in the provinces, and he is still just smiling gently and obligingly at her, she finally gives up and goes home with her girlfriend, and he yet again feels that inexpressible relief when something, the ultimate, the most sublime, has for a moment been possible, when all you have to do is reach out but you didn't, and now it is definitively too late, and everything will again just be the same life, which never begins, and in the crowd of ten-, twenty- and thirty-year-long inebriations blearily and incoherently jostling him up to the bar, as if they were his future, he suddenly sees her come sweeping back in, she grabs him firmly by the jaw and kisses him, and done is done, and this is where the story begins.

He is lying at her side in the darkness of the basement under the farmhouse listening to her breathing, which even in her sleep is as blissful as life relishing itself. He places a hand on her skin, it is damp and soft and yielding, swaying, as if the flesh isn't firm, but a dark liquid, a heavy water, allowing his hand to sink in and vanish. He thinks her name and she wakes up, and he asks if he's

dangerous, the stepfather, if he'll soon be so humiliated
and pitiful that he'll no longer see himself as a human
being, and will suddenly grab the rifle and without any
kind of scene or demonstration of power just fire away at
them all, the mother, her, the little brothers and, of
course, last but not least, himself, splatter the back of his
head across the wall, and she mumbles that it's the
middle of the night, I'm sleeping, and then sinks back
into sleep. He lies there for a long time, listening, then
he lifts the duvet and steps out onto the cold cement
floor; he reaches his hands out into the darkness, which
here in the basement under the farmhouse on a winter's
night in February or early March really is—unlike the
suburban residential neighborhoods dazzled by the
glare of a streetlamp on the other side of the bushes—the
darkness no human being has ever seen. And here, in
this sleepless darkness, time and happenings merge, he
is both the slender young boy feeling his way through
the sleeping house and the old woman who, when telling
her tale decades later, creates the "white farmhouse" as
a mythical place from what has been definitively lost,
and, using her seven senses in the language, scrabbles it
out from the dark materials of memory: the bookcase,
the wall with its couple of tattered posters, the windowsill and door leading to what he (or she) comatosely la-
bels the boiler room, where the air is thick and
"suffocatingly" hot, somewhere ahead to the left he (or
she) finds the door to the staircase, which is narrow and

just a winding shaft up to what from the outside looks like the door to a broom cupboard hidden under the more elegant staircase leading up to the second floor, like a shift in language he walks through the entrance hall and into the smallest room, which recollection has already transformed to her room, this night the "white farmhouse" is not a place in time, but a narrative room after room after room, where everything and every movement can occur precisely when it should, her big iron bed with its footboard of square metal tubing on which he cuts his thigh, making it sting and blood trickle down over his knee, to the right the big wardrobe, dusty-green or dark-blue and bulging open from inside by her vast assortment of clothes, in all of which she always looks the same, but which will turn him, who is anybody, into almost anyone else, toreador, doll, hooker, captain, and in the bed behind him under crumpled duvets they both lie naked or half un- or dressed, day and night, through dusk and dawn, it's as if they'll never get out of that bed and get going with life, and the mother comes in and says it's already late afternoon, Stina! in her slightly strident warm animated and cultured voice, you'll end up pregnant! and then she laughs and disappears, and the girl gets pregnant, of course she does, but not now, not until later when "the endless summer" comes to an abrupt end, he opens the double door and steps into the large and it being February icy-cold room, where forever sitting in the armchair to the right in the glow from a floor lamp is Aunt Janne, even while living her life with her American professor of philosophy, "Uncle Bob," on the other side of the Atlantic in Massachusetts, and even while seeing him for the first time, in a long line of vestment-clad young priests on their way in through the vast expanse of St. Peter's Basilica, as he turns his face away from the order of the line and sees her standing to the right of the entrance in the crowd in front of La Pietà, and even while coming to a halt straight-backed with responsibility and lightning destiny in front of him in the little room in the maternal grandmother's apartment on the second floor of a yellow building built in the nineteen-fifties in the town of Bogense, she sits forever here in the armchair in the glow from the floor lamp and makes something that sounds like a late-nineteenth-century speech, from Queen Victoria's day, a speech in her father's spirit about duty and morality and responsibility and future, manners, shame, and the dignified life to the two sitting on the sofa on the other side of the low coffee table holding hands and looking at her in astonishment, the girl boiling with respect and rebellion and him not knowing whether to swoon or laugh and not daring to look at the mother, who is sitting with a luminously aristocratic straight back to the left of her older sister and perhaps at this very moment is looking at him with the expression that will either save him or annihilate him, to white noise and dust. But not yet, none of what is going to happen is yet possible or even imaginable, there is just the night and the farmhouse, "the white farmhouse," the empty icy-cold rooms in which he has never met a living soul, nor does he now, when all the dramatis personae are asleep and only he and their personae and white flickering shadows move through yet another room and out into a sort of conservatory, empty except for a light-gray carpet of the type only usually found in municipal schools built in the nineteen-seventies, and on the carpet, one late afternoon or evening, the younger of the little brothers is sitting with a drum kit, a selection of upside-down cardboard boxes, and he kneels down and picks up the sticks, which are probably just bits of wood or back-to-front wooden spoons, and shows the boy various simple rhythms, and the boy bangs away and he tells the little boy that he'll learn alright, as long as he practices, every day, play the drums for at least a quarter of an hour, and he promises the boy and himself to make it a habit, twice a week they'll sit here, first with the cardboard boxes and later with real drums, one fine day they'll play to-gether in their own little band, and then he stands up and turns his back to the boy and never returns, neither to the cardboard boxes nor the conservatory, none of the things he promises himself or dreams about will ever come to anything, while all the things he has never wished for or promised himself will happen and amount to all there has been, his life, he opens the door to a kind of scullery and walks through it into the kitchen, the

actual stage in the house and the entire farmhouse, now
empty, dark and deserted, like the proscenium stage in a
village hall the night after a Monday in February, a faint
cold smell of supper hanging in the air and following
him out to the entrance hall and on up the stairs to the
second floor where the only toilet in the house is located.
He stops for a moment there in the darkness, the door to
the two little brothers' room behind him, and straight
ahead, just two or three meters away, the door leading
into the inner sanctum, the bedroom, in which he will
never dare set his bare feet, but just once, just one single
time in his life, with bated breath, he will *look* into it, but
not now, not until "the endless summer," to which he is
at this very moment standing on the threshold, a time
that isn't a time but the opposite of time, time's annul-
ment, in which everything, just like nature, the leaves on
the trees, the lilac, and the clouds of cherry in Jardin
Villemin, will open up and let him look into and smell
the dream that the mother will suddenly live out, now
with a completely different man, the only one who will
ever measure up to the stallion, a young Portuguese, an
artist like Caravaggio, who with his mute lips (and teeth)
will make his marks in the mother's skin, marks for the
indecent, that which is beyond the shame and the taboo,
the mark of the beautiful, the sublime, and impossible
(just a young man, a year or two younger than he is, in
every respect: the impossible), and many years later,
when he has long since been an old woman and has no

other urges than language and death, he will think that it isn't life that is a dream, it's language, narrative, this whole story *is a tale told by an idiot, full of sound and fury, signifying* . . .

Without warning, the stepfather is standing in front of him, a ghost, a shadow of himself. What the hell are you doing here, in the middle of the night? he says in his sickly nasal and bitter voice. Nothing, the young boy mumbles, I just needed a pee. The stepfather snorts derisively and walks past him down the stairs. He stands still in the darkness, listening to the stepfather's footsteps continuing through the kitchen and out to the scullery. This is it, he thinks, in a moment it'll be too late, he's the only other one awake and that's why he's here at all, that's the reason he came into the world at all, this world, in which he actually has no role to play, this isn't about him or his love affair, it's about them, this is the moment he should enter the room in which he's never going to set his bare feet, and wake the mother and get her up, and the two little brothers in the room behind him, silently fetch the girl from the basement and get all of them out into the mother's rusty-green old crate of a van, which no one in a suburban residential neighborhood would either own or have or be seen in, and, headlights off, trundle along the avenue and away from this accursed place, this "white farmhouse," which is not only haunted, but will haunt people both in and outside this story. But he does nothing, he stands rooted in the darkness listening for what is to come, the little click from the cocking of the rifle, footsteps from the scullery back through the kitchen and up the stairs. But nothing happens, not a sound, just darkness.

It's true. He did nothing. Nor did he go down to the basement and join the sleeping girl under the duvet. What happened there? At a stroke, it is daytime, the trees unfold their leaves in the May light, the dandelions in the field open their glistening yellow umbels and are white clouds lifted by the breeze and carried away, the stepfather has gone, never will he see him again *in all his life*, the girl has already moved all her things up to the smaller of the two rooms, the one facing the yard, and transformed it into her girl's room with its pink and fairy-dust glow of illusion that is the new epoch, "the endless summer" where time does not exist and space spreads and fills everything, "the white farmhouse" is the whole world, and he is never going to leave it, once a day at a pinch, perhaps every other day, take a few steps out into the yard, this cauldron of quivering light, lean against the whitewashed wall of the stables, close his eyes and feel it burn, occasionally in steaming summer rain along with the other young boy, the girl's best friend, the handsome Lars, who has long since moved in with his lovely limbs and lazy movements, the dangling arms and the feet he places on the ground as if an invisible hand is lifting it up under him, walk a few more meters in the wet grass toward the woodshed, where they don't have to chop and split what has to be chopped and split, but just each carry an armful of logs indoors for the woodburner or stove, the location of which he no longer knows and thus will never again know, and another day when he suddenly and simultaneously alone and with the girl has strayed to the other side of the barn . . . but there's nothing, what could there be out there? a field is a field is a field, the spell breaks and the old world begins, but the old world must not begin, we remain in "the endless summer" which, like Paradise, is the place that has never been and can never be revisited, only in the tale, and each day is the first, the last, and always the same: the mother comes down from the second floor leaving the bedroom door open behind her, the little brothers are playing in passionate disagreement out in the yard, the big one, who as in all archetypical pairs of brothers is the gentle one, slightly timid, weeps, the little one, who looks like his missing father, is silent and sulky, has shorter limbs and a firm and righteous gaze (like a teacher of the old school or the boy who became an adult at too early an age), within the chilly shadow in the iron bed lie the girl and the slender boy, who is more likely a girl, both talking at the same time just to hear their own voices, their life is the life everlasting, and they waste it away recklessly and on nothing at all, while the mother, whose aimlessness has a completely different kind of firmness and form, like the perfect wheel turning

its light out of empty space, picks out the stallion's
hooves, grooms it, saddles up and puts on the bridle,
mounts, and rides out for the whole day and brings it
back in the twilight and feeds it, waters it, and hears it
snort in the darkness when she closes the stable door
behind her and walks into the kitchen and lights the
candle that will burn down while they eat and stay at the
table talking into the night, there is music, but no memory of radio or television, no news broadcast, every day
is the same day and just as startling, and its time is that
of music, whose premise and element is the time it sus-
pends, world history is their movement and the totality
they see without looking for anything, nothing will happen, life will be sheer expectancy, an expectancy with no
object, expectancy of nothing, the delight of expectancy
per se, every movement is an event, late in the evening,
when the mother's rusty-green van with commercial li-
cense plates drives up the avenue, the two little brothers,
the girl, and the two young boys, handsome Lars and the
oh so fine and slender boy, have to draw themselves up
from the forbidden trunk space at the back of the van
after the long drive along highways and byways across
the flat land, and will forever see the cones of light strik-
ing the whitewashed gable of the stables and the wire
mesh in front of it and above the coughing of the engine
will hear the twelve almost newly-hatched chickens, all
roosters, crowing powerfully and yet drowsily, as if they
were the heralds assigned to announce Peter's denial but

had overslept and woken up abruptly in a tutti to Judgment Day. And where have they been? Places that, just like them, are beyond time, to dinner, perhaps, with the occult "hair artist" at work on the second floor of his father's old general store out by the coast, in the little town with the set of traffic lights, a full-bearded, fattish manikin who is perhaps, when observed from the other world, in his early thirties, but in this world seems to have been taken from a late self-portrait by Rijn van Rembrandt, his low-ceilinged second-floor dwelling is bathed in that everlasting brownish simmering darkness into which the last drop of light (from a taper we can't see), with its implication of the last of humankind, is sucked. No daytime here, and the darkness is room after room after room heaving with shelves of books, dust, and occult objects, and, furthest in at the far end, a kitchen—also just dimly lit-up by tapers—recalling the manic Strindberg's alchemical laboratory in Paris with its simmering and bubbling and reeking flasks, or rather colossal pots and ovens and frying pans over which the bearded manikin is bending, assisted by the handsome youth, who moves in with him every so often as a kind of sorcerer's apprentice, the subsequent dinners are orgies of heavy wines and dripping juicy joints of beef, browned ducks, pigeons, snails, frogs, and stuffed pheasants, the gnawed bones and carcasses of which are not piled on the plates and carried out to the kitchen, but simply thrown over the shoulder through the always-open window and down through the night to yard and street. The orgies and the alchemical laboratory (experiments in melting down dead animals to a higher matter) are financed by an advance on the inheritance from his father's general store and royalties from the lyrics he at times, and happily during dinner with a half-gnawed pigeon carcass in the one hand and a grease-dripping ballpoint pen in the other, writes for washed-up or from the outset failed Danish pop singers who perform them in competition with one another (a final dying echo of the conception of European culture at the Athenian competitions for best tragedy in the theater of Ancient Greece) at the annual national heats of the Eurovision Song Contest. And at the furthest reaches of night, when the heavy wines have had their effect, he inveigles them to have large and the longest possible tufts of their hair cut off, which he will then braid together, the slender young boy's with the girl's and later also the mother's with the Portuguese artist's, in lovely, magical necklaces and bracelets and earrings, which they will each wear as talismans in a sealing of the love that is also a curse (like the war that gives life to history, but is deadly to people). One morning the girl makes another last attempt to catch the bus that will take her into the slightly larger town in time to see her friends go home from upper secondary school, but of course fails; her best friend, the ideal of a Nordic-handsome youth Lars, can't even be bothered to try, he stays in the kitchen with his milky

coffee or rises in a pleasurable motion for the sake of
appearances and sits outside on the red-hot doorstep and
closes his eyes against the sun, and if the mother, who is
otherwise now free and can live her life unseen by detectives and men who fear (and therefore despise) women,
still occasionally drives all the way over to the provincial
capital on the mainland in order to take some courses or
sit an exam at the university there, well, that's beyond
the grasp of the story. "The endless summer" has started,
but the moment at which there is no going back, the
point of no return, has yet to occur. But here comes the
prelude:

One day the girl must have managed to get to her school
anyway, because in the late afternoon she comes back
and sits in the kitchen with the others and tells them that
the girl she sits next to has been visited by her Portuguese pen pal José and his friend, also called José, who
have taken leave of absence from their schools and have
hitchhiked all the way up through Europe to see the light
over Skagen and stay a few nights with the friend and
her parents in their small detached house; but now that
they have finally arrived, and the girl's parents have seen
that they are not just innocent postcards but two real,
very young men, and not of the reliably lighter type, but
the darker and more unreliable sort they have possibly
seen while on a vacation package to Majorca or, why not,
the Canary Islands, they won't have them in their house

after all, and certainly not at night, and the mother, who just then comes in from the stables, stops in the doorway and loosens her muddy-green hairband and tosses her head, ivory-colored hair sweeping through the light and down over her shoulders, and says that the girl should telephone her friend and say that the two young men or boys can come out here, before midnight, and sleep on the floor in the sitting room, for a night or three, whereupon she turns and walks up the stairs to take a bath. And shortly after midnight, the two Portuguese arrive with their rucksacks, the one, the pen pal, actually not so dark at all, far from it, tall and strong and with golden curls, Peixe, he is called, "The Fish," but where he comes from they call him "o Vikingo," the other one is smaller but equally masculine, dark and mysterious, a little shy like a wild cat, the same soundless movements, an abrupt laughter cracking his face in a flash of light that has disappeared before you have seen who he is. They unroll their sleeping bags on the floor in the sitting room, and the mother comes in and says hello, polite and aloof, bids them welcome and vanishes up into her bedroom. And they spend the following nights and days at the farm, fit into its rhythm, don't get anywhere, don't see any of the things they had planned to see, just sleep, wake and laze around in the sunlit yard, sit in the kitchen until late at night and dip chunks of bread into the milky coffee, the red wine, laugh at the same nothing as the girl and the two young boys, while the mother, aloof as a queen, lives her life on the periphery of the circle and just occasionally, once the horse has been watered, twilight brought back in, and the little brothers put to bed, sits in the candlelight glow around the table listening to their voices, she is thirty-four, her daughter has just turned seventeen, and the boys at the table are eighteen, nineteen, and twenty. On the morning of the third or fourth day, the two Portuguese roll up their sleeping bags and carry their rucksacks out to the van, and while the five older children exchange hugs and addresses and promise one another all the things young people always promise one another and hardly ever carry through—to write, meet, never forget—the mother starts the van and then drives the two Portuguese to the main road and drops them off so they can hitch across the country and maybe by late evening arrive in time to see the light hanging on into the night over Skagen. She turns the van around and drives back to the farm, and "the endless summer" carries on as if nothing had happened and nothing ever will. At dusk one evening, they all climb into the rusty-green van and, now a couple of hours late—the kind of lateness caused neither by busyness nor disaster, but by nothing and absence of time—drive to another occult dinner with the so-called hair artist in the little town. On the way, they pass the spot where, on a morning that already seems to belong to a completely different life in another world, but happened to be the morning of that same day, the mother had dropped off the two Portuguese, and they're still standing there. The mother brakes, and reverses the hundred meters to the two young men, who at first just stare vacantly, as if the motorist must have braked because of a puncture and it can't possibly have anything to do with them, and then finally recognize the van. The girl rolls the window down and they say they've been standing there ever since, for nearly twelve hours, and in the course of the day a representative section of the nation's population and their cars has driven past, but not one has stopped and picked them up. The girl looks at her mother and the mother leans across the elder of the little brothers and opens the door, asks the little brother to climb into the back and tells the two Portuguese to get in. Then she turns the car around and drives back to the farm. And while the two exhausted Portuguese boys sit in the kitchen eating the supper leftovers, bread and the last slices of cheese, she telephones the so-called hair artist and tells him they won't be making it, something has come up, and they'll have to come maybe some other day or night. She then walks back into the kitchen and looks at them. She is no longer aloof, she is angry, like a queen disgraced by her people. She says they should unpack their things again, the sitting room and the entire farm is theirs, they can stay as long as they like, a month, the rest of their lives, if need be. And so the die is cast. And perhaps it's just that the four of them—the slender boy and the handsome youth, the Portuguese "Vikingo" and, not least, the

girl—are too young to understand her words as anything
other than an expression of hospitality, maybe both she
and the younger of the two Portuguese boys, the small,
dark, reticently intense one, without yet having so much
as looked one another in the eye, hardly exchanged a
word, know what has happened and that there is no going
back. A moment, seven, twenty years later, he has married
again, to a slightly younger compatriot, a dark and melancholy girl who throws herself from their balcony with
its view across the old Alfama and the Atlantic Ocean;
the mother has withdrawn into solitude in a little townhouse near the coast in northern Sealand, together with
the male who has accompanied her as a lover throughout
the preceding six lives with six utterly different males, of
whom several are long since dead—of bitterness, kidney
failure, obesity, self-hatred—the stallion; the ideal of a
Nordic-fair youth Lars with the shapely hands and feet
has turned to dust, moisture and calcium under a grave-
stone in a wind-swept, slightly sloping cemetery on the
outskirts of a provincial town after a funeral at which the
other seven are present but silent, unable to say a word,
while a cousin of the same age, making a speech, the final
nod, calls the early death the punishment of a righteous
god. And the girl? the slender young boy? the two little
brothers? o Vikingo? We'll come back to them.

Time passes, and time doesn't pass, it is "the endless
summer," the two young Portuguese have now moved

into and become part of, indefinitely, "the rest of your lives, if need be." By now they are a little colony numbering too many to fit into the rusty van, they leave it where it is and really don't go anywhere, not even out to the little town on the coast, dinner at the so-called hair artist's place is allowed to sit and rot like one of those "nature mortes" in paintings by Rembrandt the elder's Flemish colleagues, which far from being "morte" teem with mites, flies, and drops of the dew of purification, only the mother occasionally drives in and visits her mother and does a spot of shopping for the orgy of milk, bread, and wine, semisoft table cheese and leeks from the neighbor's field (no soft-boiled breakfast egg, no fried egg in the dusk, from twelve crowing roosters in the cage by the gable), which is the miracle of which life on the farm is composed and for which she is by and large the only one who pays, using the child support money that the just a few months ago long-since-missing stepfather (against his will, but forced to by the system) transfers to her account. Life at "the white farmhouse" starts to resemble the stuff of which dreams are made, like life a century earlier in the so-called artists' colony at Skagen (the light of which the two Portuguese *never ever* arrived to see), a life that is simultaneously in the midst of and completely beyond time, a world of its own, apart from the fact that life in the colony at "the white farmhouse" has no higher purpose, no ideas or ideals of the sublime, of symbols, of composition, of community and everyday life, no dreams, in life as dream. Their lives are one life, they get up in the same day and go to sleep in the same night. The only one who, like the mother, seems to have a life outside the community is the younger of the two Portuguese, the small dark one who is quite clearly also the poorest. His movements are soft and self-assured, not trying to be someone, he just *is*, a self-confident incarnation of the pride we, without having encountered it before, recognize as the pride a country or maybe rather a culture might have, and which is its very existence and survival in the physical body of its people beyond any economic system and completely independent of whether the state in which it is currently occurring endures or goes bankrupt and is placed under the supervision of more powerful nations and market forces, the incarnation of that Portuguese man born along with the far-reaching expeditions of discovery in the late fifteenth-century and who later voyaged through history as conqueror, seducer, poet, aristocrat. His shoes and clothes are threadbare hand-me-downs from older brothers, uncles, at any rate they have certainly been worn by others before him, but everything is always clean and looks freshly ironed, put together with a discreet but expert sense of colors and the tactility of fabrics. He knows who he is, unlike the others who—apart from his two-years-older buddy, "o Vikingo," who after consultation with his father, the patriarch of the family, has reached the idea that when he returns from his trip to Denmark in early autumn, he will embark on some form of natural science course—don't know who they are, or what to do with their lives, and therefore in a sense are nothing other than the very life they are living here and now in "the endless summer." Perhaps that is what makes him—even though he is the youngest but one, the girl being a year younger—the only adult, the only man. From time to time he vanishes without a word and stays away for half or whole days and comes back with a drawing, a sketch, or a watercolor of a church or a manor house that none of the others, apart from the mother, have ever seen or had any idea existed. He doesn't say much and never tells them anything about himself, so the other one, the two-years-older and obviously wealthier buddy, "o Vikingo," tells them his story. Vikingo is clearly proud of him, and you get the feeling that he has brought him along and maybe also paid for some of the trip in order to show him off and tell of him: he's an artist, from a poor background, of course, discovered or found inadvertently one morning by the little provincial town's (only) rich man, on the town square where the then eight- or perhaps ten-year-old boy, whose own family can't afford to send to school, sits drawing whatever the passersby want to see, to earn his living and that of the family, mother, father, grandmother, and the twelve older and younger siblings, who all live together in two rooms in the basement of a house in one of the oldest neighborhoods—where the town's poorest live and rent out their basements to the even poorer families, the slightly darker, more restless, unsettled, untrustworthy, those with gypsy blood in their veins, basements entered via the narrowest of passages in the network of narrow passages in the densely built-up area of small houses—with kitchen and hencoop in one and the same cement room, separated by wire mesh with a quivering door, made of the same wire mesh stapled to a rough wooden frame, which is always open so the hens can move freely between the kitchen and a chicken yard devoid of sun and partially concealed under the little cement bridge that takes the wealthier families on the first floor across and down to the little sunny backyard in which they grow their own vegetables and flowers, and having stood for half an hour in the shade of the fashionable Italian hat with its silk band that he, being the richest man in the town, always wears (along with the silver-mounted cane with ivory handle on which he is at this moment resting his hands), contemplating the little boy's astonishing sketches (which those few of the other town residents who take any notice whatsoever of the boy, and perhaps even let him draw their silhouette or that of their young daughter, do not view as anything other or more than a poverty-stricken lad's venerable attempt to earn a respectable coin or two, unlike the older brothers in the family who, as everyone in the little town knows, only leave home—thereby giving the younger brothers just a bit more room in the bed, in the furthest back of the two rooms in which they all sleep crisscross every night—on the day they are sent to prison for the first time), the rich man decides then and there to be the boy's patron, first paying for his schooling and private lessons with the town's greatest (and only) artist, and later funding his studies, which he embarks upon when just fourteen or fifteen years of age, at the art academy in the capital, Lisbon, eighty kilometers southwest, out by the sea. He is the only one in the little colony at "the white farmhouse" who spends the time it takes each morning to polish his shoes, which are not tennis shoes or sneakers like the other three boys wear, but classic light-brown men's shoes, well-worn but well-maintained, with laces and leather soles. And when, late in the evening, he comes walking as if out of mere nothing across the fields toward the farmhouse, they can already recognize him at a great distance by the hat, which is not a patron-hat but, of course, a very slightly more "personal" and broad-brimmed hat, and so even or perhaps especially in the sharp light over the flat, north Funen fields it is obvious, merely from the silhouette, that "there goes an artist."

One day, nonetheless, one of the two Danish boys, the oh so fine and slender one, has been into town and brought back the friend with whom he shared a room in the life he has now dropped out of. The friend, a lanky lad from Odense, who the others also see as an artist, is attracted to the Portuguese and maybe in particular to the certitude he carries with him, a glow of the "lightning destiny" that the Odense lad and his artist-dreaming friends in the provincial town long for and often talk about, but have never personally felt or seen in the older artists they occasionally visit but only know from an almost century-old poem, the point of which is precisely this: that the lightning destiny is no longer possible, it is over and done with, a destiny both he and his friends would be not merely happy about, but would be redeemed, liberated and definitively determined by, and would display with pride, but which the young Portuguese simply carries as a matter of course. The Portuguese takes the lanky Odense lad with the prematurely receding hairline, the broad beak-like nose and long loose-jointed arms, the source of his nickname "Twiggy," along on his walks across the fields, and late in the evenings they return to the farmhouse and the kitchen with sketches and charcoal drawings and sit together in the candlelight glow with omelet, chunks of bread, and wine, talking about the light in the old masters and madness and the *intensity* in Van Gogh. One day, in return, the lanky lad takes the Portuguese along to show him the town, or perhaps it's more a case of parading the young Portuguese and his lightning destiny and the glow it casts upon him personally in the local graphic studio, where he himself is the young hope in whom the older artists—who have long since abandoned the dream of revolutionizing the world through their art and are resigned to the safety found in being part of a small community where everyone knows everyone and they all go to one another's private viewings and are more or less evenly spread across the local selection committees deciding who can exhibit this year as artist of the year or "Funen resident of the year" at the local public museum of art—see a trace of the dream of a lightning destiny that they themselves once had, and have therefore given him unrestricted access to machines and materials in the graphic studio they run together, with municipal support, and in which he and the young Portuguese now drop out of the world, and from which they do not return until several days later to the farmhouse and the kitchen, carrying etchings, woodcuts, and drypoint prints. The lanky, somewhat nervy and restless Odense lad, who despite his obsession with art never really comes to believe in his own talent, is now part of life at "the white farmhouse," but at the same time he carries on with his life in the other world, occasionally goes to the graphic studio or visits older artists who have moved out to the countryside, living in forest ranger houses or hunting lodges they rent from the local estate owners, and with whom he spends several sleepless days and nights drinking home-distilled apple and plum brandy and discussing art and writers, Durrell's Alexandria Quartet and Avignon Quintet (not a word about the contemporaneous and zeitgeisterly new wave, not a word about punk and an unruliness and a rebellion far beyond rock music, not a word about the pure noise and the ecstasy of destruction), and in the course of the summer, which in the world outside the farmhouse is not endless, but totally natural with a culmination, a midsummer evening and a late summer, he gets a place at the local art academy, and a couple of years later he holds his first exhibition in the capital, at a café. The central exhibit, "Hysteric"—a multicolored and wild and very yellow intaglio print of a grotesquely-distorted female with his own bony limbs, oblong skull, and, in the golden section, a big toe with a luminous red nail, transparent, trembling like a jelly slab atop the cream-filled discs of a confectioner's cookie—takes on a mythical quality among the survivors of "the endless summer," and later in life he never surpasses it, the lightning from the jelly slab becomes his destiny.

Abruptly, "the endless summer is over," the lanky lad leaves the town and moves to the capital city and together with a slightly younger and far more purposeful friend, a young Jew who does tai chi, is a black belt, and has spent a year with his master in Beijing or Shanghai, he takes over the running of a small art school and for the next few years these two, along with their pupils and possibly without him really realizing, live the synthesis of art and life that the twentieth-century avant-gardes and in particular the second, the nineteen-sixties' avant-garde, and the situationists prophesied as their version of the twentieth-century Utopia. He moves into and lives his life in the studio's new world, and everything they do there, every movement and the things, forms and phenomena produced by these movements, are equal portions art, life, and world; instead of washing the dishes, they look at them, move the elements around, arrange them in new shapes, gaze into the pan of rice and the last pinch of curry powder as if this is the new world before they eat it, and the act of consuming it is a gesture, a "throw," an in-it-iation, a quantum leap out of time and into a completely different, seventh dimension, a completely different notion of existence and community, rice and curry, the collision of the white, almost chalk-white of the rice, no, more like the white flesh of the codfish on the white plate, yes, the North Sea, the ocean, the unknown icy-cold depths, the last white patch on the planet, eleven kilometers below the surface of the sea, and the intense desert-dust-burning, globe-core-searing yellow of the curry. Art is life, and life is art. At any rate, that's what it's like for him. The slightly younger friend, the Jewish tai chi expert, is more pragmatic, he is well aware that the synthesis of art and life, of work and creation, is not a Utopia, a proposal for a new and better world and a new and better human community, but a strategy in the one world that exists. He intuitively understands that his personal selling-point must be his incorruptibility and his radicality. After a couple of years, this younger friend wins a place at the Royal Danish Academy of Fine Arts, and while still a student he is

taken on by one of the most important international gallerists in the city, the works in his first exhibition, the
prices set unusually high, already get sold out at the
private viewing, museums abroad phone in to secure,
whatever the price, one of the paintings they haven't
even seen yet, just heard the buzz about. In the subsequent interviews, published in newspapers and art journals, he tells his story as a myth, his tai chi classes turn
into a past in "Chinese boxing," and his Jewish background—with strong family ties, rituals, the historical
weight that no ordinary citizen in the country embodies,
but can only envy or try to identify with in novels, poems
and plays, the brother who has moved back to Israel, life
in conflict between two cultures, two identities—becomes
a commodity on the art market, a signature he ensures
isn't too "authentic" by transforming the authentic surname with its Yiddish-German ring and vocal ornamen-
tation to a single letter of the alphabet, a personal
symbol, an R, as historyless as The Market will allow a
commodity to be. Soon he is transporting himself around
alternately on a carrier cycle with his two lovely children,
like a young artist with great "integrity," or, like a shooting star, in the Jaguar on which he has spent a half or a
quarter of his first million, while the other, slightly older
and now former buddy, the lanky Odense lad with the
ever-more-receding hairline, hauls his rusty bicycle up to
the second floor and into the studio he now inhabits all
by himself—without his buddy and without pupils—and

tries to fix the bike chain back on, and apart from that doesn't go anywhere, on the contrary, he stays living in the studio, but his paintings and sculptures and traces of the life lived no longer have the grotesque and trembling lump of jelly on the big toe of the "Hysteric," or the "shock of the new" as triggered by the gaze into the pan of rice. Instead of letting things be what they are, and work on arranging their forms, he starts seeing them as symbols, and instead of just talking about the mad expressionists, about Munch, Nolde, and Schiele, he tries to paint like them, which of course merely results in symbol-laden Nolde-like anachronisms, paintings that no one has the patience to look at. One day, he has suddenly abandoned his own belief in art, or at least the notion of himself as artist. He's going to make films instead. He spends several months writing a screenplay about two men walking through a flat landscape, across fields and along gravel roads, one of them staring relentlessly at the horizon and what might be beyond it while the other just stares down at the ground ahead, at everything there is and is passing by. But the film never comes to anything. Instead, he meets a woman, has two children, and moves with them like a little family into the second floor of an old detached house in one of the capital city's run-down outlying suburbs, and you can occasionally encounter this lanky, now aging Odense lad with the two children in the front carrier of the bicycle, like a proper family man. All at once, he has moved out, takes

a bit of work as a graphic designer, and one morning like
so many other mornings when sitting on a bench in a
park or next to one of the city lakes, he gets into conversation with a slightly older man who shows him a book
he absolutely must read. Soon you can be sure to meet
him or be overtaken by him when walking across City
Hall Square, like a head clerk who, having been absent
for half a century, suddenly reappears in a completely
wrong era with his boring brownish gabardine trousers,
his boring brown shoes and a boring dark-blue windbreaker, and, after a quick hi and "how are things with
you," yet again tries to give you a copy of the book you
absolutely must read (about sin, evil and Jesus Christ,
the Son of God who is the only one who can save humankind from its state of perdition, and so forth). From
time to time, he is still visited by his two children in the
small dark three-room apartment he has moved into
temporarily, with its toilet off the back staircase, but
when his mother falls ill he moves home to be with her
and his father in the small detached house on the outskirts of the provincial town he had left twenty years
earlier, because he had wanted to live a completely different, more authentic, real and artistic life. Throughout
his childhood, his father had worked as a low-ranked
engineer in a largish company and designed solutions for
smallish units (of what? and for what? the son had never
understood), and being the youngest of three children,
the only boy, with two older sisters (who didn't become

engineers like their father or stay-at-home housewives like their mother, but, devoid of desire to do anything else, nonetheless carried on the life their parents had lived, with long-term employment, a small detached house, a husband, children, and a perfectly ordinary, cheap-to-run and not too flashy car), he had started drawing at an early age, from the very outset with the awareness that he wouldn't be drawing technical solutions to smallish units, but *visions* of other worlds and other creatures and a completely different *light*. He had more or less consciously done everything that the parents and the two older sisters didn't understand: looking at paintings, reading poems, playing the violin, and going with friends in strange clothes to strange places to hear strange music that didn't "sound like anything the rest of us know." At seventeen he had dropped out of school and left home to live his very own life as an artist. And unlike most of his friends, all of whom wanted to be artists too, but at the same time, as a precaution, would first sit their final high-school exams and perhaps, so as to have something to fall back on, start a course of further education on the side, it seemed as if he not only knew what he wanted to do, and believed in it, but also really did it. But maybe he had never managed to leave home completely, maybe he had, unconsciously, left a door ajar, quite literally: having lived in various rented rooms and shared apartments the first time round—long before the jelly slab's lightning and escape to Copenhagen—he moved into his own apartment, a rather dark, three-room, first-floor apartment in one of the provincial town's old working-class districts, it was neither his current girlfriend nor his upstairs neighbor who—just in case—had the spare key, but his parents. And at frequent intervals, when they knew he probably wasn't home, the engineer and his wife arrived in their cheap-to-run car, let themselves into their son's apartment carrying a vacuum cleaner, bucket, mop, and various cleansing agents, and started to clean, tidy, removed dried-up condoms from the floor next to the mattress, made the "bed," put books back in the shelving unit, and also cleared away the son's, the would-be artist's meticulously arranged composition of fruit, wine, glasses, and bowls on a cloth draped over a round table a few meters in front of the easel with its still only half-finished "nature morte," the disgracefully shriveled apples and mold-spotted peaches were thrown in the trash and the glasses and bowls nicely washed and put back in the cupboard above the kitchen sink. The engineer and his wife then locked the door behind them and drove home to the small detached house, and neither they nor the son ever mentioned it to one another, not a word. During the final months of his mother's life, it is now he, the lanky son, who takes care of her, washes her, feeds her, and puts her to bed, cooks dinner for his father and does the dishes, vacuums, cleans, puts everything away and tidies up after them, all three. But when at the end of her last months, which by now is half a year, the mother is finally dead and has been given a good Christian funeral, and he has done his duty as a Christian and good son and can return with a peaceful mind to life and his two children in the capital, he stays living with his father in the very run-down and dark detached house he had left twenty years earlier because it represented everything he didn't want to be and never *in his life* would become.

But all this—the jelly slab's lightning and life's unfurling as destiny and tale—is as of yet inconceivable. In this present he is still part of "the endless summer," and one day it isn't the Portuguese artist, but the slender and far-too-sensitive boy who accompanies the lanky Odense lad into town to spend a couple of days, staying with him in the room that used to be his too. One morning the girl rings from the farm and insists on speaking with her boyfriend. When he is handed the phone, she tells him that something has happened. What has happened? asks the slender young boy. She can't say. But is it something serious, has grandmother died? No no, she says, that's not it. So what is it? If something's happened, can't she just say what it is? She's not crying, she doesn't sound distraught, more like shocked, agitated. He asks if she's pregnant? Or perhaps he specifically *doesn't* ask that, he just thinks it, or tries not to think it. Is it something serious? he asks. But she doesn't answer that question. Then he realizes she really *can't* say it, she can't even think it.

It's to do with Mom, she says, Mom and . . . In the evening, when he returns to the farm, he can sense it, from the moment he steps in through the doorway and stands in the entrance hall. Everything looks like it usually does, the same slightly dusty, elegant disarray (shadows and light), but the whole house is charged, quivering. Everything goes on as it usually does, the mother makes an omelet with various leftovers, and they eat it with slices of sourdough rye bread in the glow of the candlelight at the round table in the kitchen. Afterward, the mother puts the two little brothers to bed, and the girl and the slender boy and the handsome Lars and the tall, curly-fair-haired "Vikingo" stay at the table while the younger of the two Portuguese, the dark one, rolls a cigarette, and stands up and paces a little back and forth in the periphery of the candlelight glow, comes to a halt by the kitchen table, looks out into the darkness, lights the cigarette and goes outside to take an evening walk, returns half an hour later and sits at the table, turned slightly away, and writes something in the tiniest writing in a notebook or makes some sketches on a sheet of paper. At night, it proves impossible to sleep, as so often before the sensitive slender boy lies awake, but whereas he usually listens to the silence in the sleeping house, he can now sense that all the others are awake too, listening. Next morning, when the girl and the slender boy and the tall curly-fair-haired Portuguese are sitting at the kitchen table in the morning sun, each cradling a cup of milky galão coffee and maybe chatting a little or not really saying anything and waiting for lazy, apparently so life-loving, wonderfully handsome Lars to appear and sit down with his forbearing sort of sighing smile, the mother comes down from the bedroom on the second floor, wearing as always the white bathrobe and with her long fair hair combed back and tightly gathered in a ponytail, and her eyes are bright and unseeing and shining with madness. She makes herself a cup of coffee, heats up the milk, pours the milk into the coffee and stirs it with a teaspoon, her movements are calm, flowing, as if they are enjoying themselves, she places the cup on the saucer and carries it over to the table and sits down and looks at them and looks through them and takes a sip of her coffee, and smiles, not at anyone in particular, and each of them knows that it is me, me alone she is secretly, unseen by the others, smiling at, a calm smile, madly, secretively luminous and bland, as if she is telling them something she herself doesn't understand, and then it is gone, as if the smile wasn't hers, but something that slid across her face, through it, and each of them thinks, without thinking it, that perhaps it was just the light, the clouds momentarily parting, and the table between them smoldering forth in an arabesque of light-shade, a quaking reflected in her face and sinking into itself. A little later, the dark young Portuguese comes down, he too as usual already dressed, shirt, waistcoat, trousers, the shoes, which in a moment he will take out and polish sitting in the sun on the doorstep, are dangling from two fingers of his hand. He doesn't sit with the others and he doesn't eat anything, doesn't even pour a cup of coffee, but that's not unusual, he often doesn't eat anything until sometime in the afternoon, maybe he takes an apple along on his morning walk; he rolls a cigarette, paces a little back and forth while turning the cigarette between his fingers, he doesn't smile, nor does he look at the others, nor does he look away, he *is*, and just like the mother he is radiant, but not like the sun, it is an invisible radiance that can only be seen by the bodies of the others, an intense, wild, and tightly reined radiance, as if he alone is composed of pulsating blood. And the day passes, as the day always passes, the mother goes out to her horse (somewhat later than usual), the little brothers play, argue, fight, the four youngsters laze about, and he, the younger Portuguese, the dark one with the elegant hands, the long fingers he likes to spread, gather, spread again, so you are drawn to looking at them and as soon as you've looked away you want to look at them again because you cannot get enough of looking at them, the way they spread so the thin skin between them is stretched, "whitens," and is gathered again, pleasurably, stretched and gathered, sits on the doorstep in the sun and polishes his shoes, puts them on, stands up and takes an apple from the bowl and drops it into the waistcoat pocket and disappears across the fields and doesn't return until dusk. And for the rest of the evening and night and for the days, evenings, and nights to come, they are all a little quieter than usual, going about their business without looking at each other, eyes cast slightly downward, sliding to evade one another's gazes, each smiling quietly, filled with an almost unbearable delight, but without saying anything, without talking about or even mentioning "it," they don't have to, they know that the others know that they know, filled with a happiness that isn't theirs, but is also not the mother's or the Portuguese youth's, a happiness that is the world's happiness. And every morning, and every morning just slightly later, perhaps just a couple of minutes, so the day starts to tilt, and "the endless summer" sets off into a quivering slide, the mother walks out of the bedroom against the light from the east-facing window, in her bathrobe, her long ivory-colored hair combed back and gathered tightly in a ponytail with the muddy-green hairband, and chewed lips and shining eyes, not "wild," more like mad or shocked, but not at the Portuguese youth or at herself, but shaken by the passion, that it can be so intense, devouring, that it becomes carnivorous, cannibalistic. And when they encounter her, by chance, on the stairs, on the way through the entrance hall or in the kitchen, they have to cast their eyes downward because it is too much, too intense (and at the same time joyful, making them want to laugh, to rejoice), and she knows it and bears it, aristocratically, as if nothing has happened, carries on as usual, puts the kettle on to make coffee, heats the milk, pours it, stirs it with the teaspoon and drinks, slowly, pleasurably, terrified, and without sitting at the table, she simply can't. And behind her, like a rearing shadow, or not until a few minutes later, along he comes, the just seventeen- or nineteen-year-old Portuguese youth, *the man* who is the cause of and has done all this, which they cannot put into words, brazen, silent, proudly striding down the stairs and into the kitchen, now almost and only just almost smiling in the way and with the self-assured masculine delight only possible in a southern European, um homem machão. And the others look at him, and he looks them in the eye, and it is they who have to smile and then quickly (smiling) look away. And so the days go on, in joy, quivering, and all partake in breaking of the bread, eat it and drink the milky coffee and wine, consume each of the daily meals as if it were the Eucharist, in silence, jubilation, and joy. At no point do they talk about *it*, they can't, what should they say? how should they say *it*? but they share it, openly now, abandoning themselves heedlessly to the days and nights, the light and darkness and movements of the body, the music they listen to, conversations about everything else just not *it*, which at the same time is the only thing they, without mentioning *it*, talk about. The only person who isn't wholeheartedly rejoicing—apart from the two small brothers who possibly sense *it* but are still too young to understand what *it* is, and even though they too see the

Portuguese youth come out of their mother's bedroom, behind her, like a menacing shadow, a sorcerer enveloped in a dark cloud, and they too react, the eldest, the hypersensitive, fair, nervy one, he falls more frequently, hurts himself, weeps, must be comforted by the mother, it *has* to be the mother, *she* has to comfort him and pick him up, the youngest, on the other hand, closes down, becomes sullen and will *not* accept the mother's hugs or cautious overtures—is the daughter, she can't take *it* in, like the others she is also about to explode, but from desperation, as if it's *her* existence and not the mother's that is under threat, she, the young girl, the only almost-virgin in the house, she who should be the object of all four men's desire and lust and eyes, she who is meant to be hitting her stride, blossoming and beginning to live her life as woman, breaking away from her mother, she has been passed over, neglected, wiped out by her own mother, brazenly, she who needs the mother to envy her adolescence and yet acknowledge her right to that adolescence and step into the background as a solid and unshakable picture of motherliness and not an agitated, bitten-to-bits wild creature who does indeed, on stepping out of the bedroom and straight out to her two small sons and her teenage daughter, assume her aristocratic and awe-inspiring supremely lofty bearing, her queenly dignity (not for a moment is she "beside herself" or unstable, quite the contrary, she is so much inside herself and at one with herself in her aristocratic iron grip that she is about to explode), but cannot possibly hide the bitten lips and no way can she conceal her *joy* (the madly shining eyes). During the nights, it is now the young, dark, and soft girl, the daughter with the delicate bones and the large, now far too motherly breasts, who lies awake and thinks about *it* and has to wake up the young boy and talk to him about *it*, which he can't talk about, only listen to her attempts to put into words, and during the mornings and afternoons, when she, who is otherwise impossible to get out of the kitchen, bed, or her sunny spot in the yard leaning against the hot stables wall, drags him along on wandering walks along lanes, past fields of leeks, barley, potatoes, fields with piebald cattle and the occasional horse, walks during which she constantly and to his annoyance, simply from nerves, agitation, linguistic mayhem, dries up and just stands there trying to articulate something she can't identify but has to verbalize so she doesn't explode, the slender young boy can sense how her unsuccessful attempt to say *it* slowly starts to take the shape of outrage, his girlfriend is outraged, endlessly outraged at her mother, her own mother, that she is behaving like that, brazenly, like a teenager, a tart! And the slender boy has to laugh, which just makes the girl's despair deepen, her feeling of being forsaken, not just by the mother and the men's eyes, but also by him, her boyfriend, who she perhaps doesn't love and never will love, but with whom she is at least in love and by whom she has an insatiable need to be looked at and listened to and understood and, above all, taken seriously.

Now "the endless summer" unfurls and comes into bloom. They start making trips to town, expeditions of conquest perhaps, but more like triumphal processions (they have already won, the king, the queen, and the whole realm), after dinner they pile into the van, the mother at the wheel, the Portuguese youth in the passenger seat, and all the others: the two young Danish boys, the slender and the handsome, the daughter, and the two little brothers whose bedtime has been abandoned, they just go along, no matter where, no matter when, laughing as they are squashed together or pushed down under the sweeping headlights of passing (police?) cars, (the other Portuguese, the tall strong one with the fair curls, "o Vikingo," has obviously slipped out of the picture, they don't talk about him, hardly remember him any more, he's probably just gone home to his world and Time and the university course he, in consultation with his father (and maybe his older brothers or uncles) had decided to start once the summer was over sometime in September); the mother, who always drives far too fast, almost hazardously, but with such skillful conviction, at least twenty kilometers an hour faster than the traffic laws (which apply to everyone else, of course, but cannot possibly apply to them) allow, snaps the van in and out between the vehicles ahead like a yo-yo, out and then, at the very last second, dazzled by the headlights of the oncoming traffic, in again, and the Portuguese youth's explosive laughter at her side, uninhibited now, neither he, she, nor the others try to hide anything any longer, neither their joy nor, as far as the girl is concerned, the raging despair, he laughs loudly, flings his upper body and head backward so the seat jolts, and his dark-brown and in the glare of the oncoming headlights abruptly flaming mane flounces in the air. And later, when they have reached the center of town and have parked the rusty-green van in a probably not completely lawful (but cheeky, so cheeky that they have to laugh in delight as they leave it) spot, on a corner or on the edge of a motorcycle parking bay, and walk toward the café that is currently *the place to be* and the social hub of the town, where the *in* crowd come, and the façade of which is made of glass and has a protruding, greenhouse-like pavilion that illuminates the whole square out front, the way in which they, like a royal couple with their entourage, *stride* in through the glass foyer, he, the Portuguese youth, straight-backed and nonchalant with the longish chestnut-burnished hair and the long, elegant, olive-dust-colored gentleman's coat sweeping out from his back, exploding in a blaring laugh that momentarily drowns out the music and causes all the (very Danish) café guests, who are sitting scattered but compactly at small round tables all the way up and down the bar and in the rooms at either end, to turn and look toward the door, at him, he pays them no attention but merely bursts again into his brazen masculine laughter with a smile that almost seems to cast a glow across the turned faces, illuminating them, and at his side, her, the fifteen-sixteen-years-older aristocratic tall luminous woman with the strong bones and the ivory-colored hair that hangs all the way down her back, proud, but nobly restrained like a queen, and behind them, behind the king and queen, the others, the extras, the entourage.

And then, just a moment later, as if by the snapping of fingers, the wedding that is, in comparison with the wedding in *The Godfather*, modest, but nonetheless has the same opulence and lighting, the town hall, which usually reduces even the most beautiful couple and the deepest love to an errand at the post office, is, the moment they enter, transformed into a church, the municipal official is their and thereby God's humble servant, who on His behalf blesses them, her, not in white, she is not an ingenuous virgin, she is already an experienced queen, wearing a plain rosemary-gray summer dress with a shiny narrow belt around a wonderfully hour-glass waist, him in an olive-dust suit, white shirt, gray-patterned waistcoat and even a hat as elegant as the erstwhile patron's. And later the wedding feast, which does not take place at "the white farmhouse," in less than no time an eternity has passed, they are now living in a fourth-floor apartment in the provincial capital, where she has resumed her studies, but "the endless summer" goes on, the feast in the little room overflowing with light, the mother—assisted by the daughter and the wives of a couple of his friends from the local émigré community—serving a meal so simple that it surpasses even the most select wedding menus at the finest old inns or hotels in the land, and is sublime and unforgettable precisely because neither it nor the usual far-too-long speeches are what you remember afterward, but *life* itself, he in the unbuttoned white shirt and the waistcoat with its patterned front and jade-green silk back (he has thrown the jacket aside at some point), arms spread across the chair backs behind her and the girl, now his stepdaughter, laid-back in his explosive overpowering laughter, the flashing white teeth and the hair she cut the day before at the round table in the little room, shoulder-length, shiny chestnut brown, he doesn't give a helping hand at any juncture during the meal, doesn't even stand up and give the normally obligatory speech to the bride, but that doesn't matter a bit, the day and age with its equality and gender-role issues is immaterial, his very existence and the love between the two of them is so prodigious that the others are not just, as usual, happy for the bride and groom, but grateful for the opportunity to be present at and share in and be filled with love as it is on that rare occasion when you really *believe* in it. And "they," who are they? They are of course the other passengers on "the endless summer" journey, the daughter, the two small brothers, handsome Lars, and the slender and fragile one who is more likely a girl, the lanky Odense lad with the now extremely receded hairline, maybe even the other Portuguese, "o Vikingo," has traveled hence on account of the celebration, but *not* Aunt Janne, the maternal grandmother, perhaps, but *not* the older brother, the lawyer from Aalbæk, this love is of no concern to them, it is beyond their world order, "they" are just the ones they want to be, along with some of the friends he has found in the local émigré community of Portuguese and South Americans, each with his Danish woman, but none like her, nowhere near, the others' women are the ordinary social-education-worker types, often rather shapeless, clumsy, but nonetheless cheerful and distinctly Nordic women, fair-haired or freckled and blazing red-heads who go on package vacations to Greece or Spain or are backpackers hitch-hiking their way around South America for six months at a time, or are development aid-workers in Africa and return home with a Greek or South American, Middle Eastern or African man, to whom they immediately get married—also at the town hall, but more for procedural reasons because it's something that primarily has to be done so the man can get a residence permit—and have a child (rarely more than one) and then, in a year or three, divorce, after which the man sticks around in the country for a couple of years and can be seen every day and often from late morning in a café or a community center, where he hangs out with his friends, nearly all of whom are men from his own émigré community, and subsequently sooner or later gives up and returns to the country, the culture, and the language he came from. But these slightly shabby exiles and their tough women with steady employment are just bitplayers, extras, the impression of a "people" necessary to make a real queen and a real king; the men laugh loudly with him, sing in Spanish and Portuguese and drink to excess, while the women rather demonstratively exercise restraint with the wine and every so often shake their heads a little and try to make themselves heard so they can continue their conversation about the daily round and, particularly, the men, their difficulty finding work, their lack of discipline, the language they haven't yet made the effort to learn and, yes, the problems of living together with them, but, as mentioned, these women and their ineffectual men are just the necessary noise it takes in order for the sublime to materialize and ordain its state of emergency, love, that which surpasses all understanding and makes language break out into music that has no meaning, no message, but just *is*, his explosive laughter and, at his side, her loftily cool and blessing aristocracy.

And a moment later, the honeymoon, the home-taking of the bride, he, the pride and hope of the small provincial Portuguese town, who has been admitted to the distinguished art academy in Lisbon where many of the famous national artists have studied before him, and who all the boys and young men of the town, and especially his brothers, the older brothers too, look up to and admire because not only is he an eccentric artist but he is also a real man who can drink with his own people while effortlessly holding his own with the very small but distinguished company of cultured citizens in the town—and which, in addition to the patron, includes the mayor and a factory owner and the leading local latifundiário with several hundred head of cattle and fifty horses, ten of which are thoroughbreds, accompanied by their wives, of course—this beautiful young man with the elegant, feminine movements and the masculine bearing and a look in his eyes that the young girls of the town and even the little sisters dream and hope might one day catch sight of them, and now he has been away for months and finally returns from a country far up to the north, a kingdom that most of the townspeople have never heard of, and with him he brings his bride, who is not the strikingly gorgeous and gentle and shy and highly distinguished daughter of an old Portuguese family of noble rank that most of the girls had in their wildest fantasies imagined he would most likely bring home from the capital one day, but a complete stranger, a woman who, what's more, is clearly considerably older than him, and taller! and what's more—rumor has it—already has two children, two boys, back home in the country she comes from, and what's more has been *married* to another man, one of her own, but who the second she stands there in full view of them is so *alarmingly* beautiful, so tall, so fair, and not only does she have blue-green eyes, but the most enchantingly long and completely straight hair, sparkling like the finest sand and sort of sweeping across her buttocks, that every form of rumor and skepticism and envy dies away and is transformed in a kind of exhilarated twittering and chattering and enchanted giggling, and when on only her second day she unhesitatingly swings herself up onto one of the latifundiário's thoroughbred Arabian horses, a high-strung, fiery four-year-old that has hardly been broken-in yet, and rides it without a saddle, just with a cordeo, as if she was a Portuguese man, um machão de verdade, then all the local and traditional rules and gender roles and notions of the ideal wife are suspended, and even the young men who usually hang around the town square on their little motorbikes, and roll cigarettes and light them and have to light them again and rev up and judder two meters forward and raise clouds of yellow dust, are transformed into bashful, giggling, and lovestruck boys. For the subsequent days and weeks, the little provincial town is thrown into some kind of euphoria, like when a queen pays her first visit to a minor provincial town, and everyone follows her every move and the reports about her and where she has been today and what she has been doing and where she has been spotted pass from kitchen to kitchen in the destitute and even more destitute streets alike and into the few white villas behind the central square, how she has been spotted very early in the morning mounted on the horse riding down along the river, how after lunch he has taken her to a café on the square where usually only the men go, how she has drunk "uma bica" with them *standing* at the bar like them and one evening had even played billiards and drunk wine with him and one of his brothers in the hall out back used for parties, and how she also mingles with the women in the daytime, helps the young man's mother and sisters in the kitchen, cleans vegetables and plucks chickens as if she was one of them, and has soon picked up a few words and actually already speaks Portuguese. And one day he takes her along to the prison in the slightly larger neighboring town, where they visit one of his older brothers who has been mixed up in something and possibly killed a man, not intentionally but in a brawl, and the way in which she greets him without any standoffishness and speaks with him and looks him in the eye as if he was a human being, and he is that too, a good-looking man, actually, even though, unlike his younger brother, his teeth are decayed, rotting stumps around a large black gap in the top row where the front four or five have been knocked out, slightly edgy, damaged, a violent, unpredictable, and brittle person constantly twitching his head and glancing to the right where there is nothing, but she just laughs loudly with him and the handsome younger brother who is her husband, and, while they are sitting there talking and

laughing, the news spreads down the corridors, from cell
to cell and passed on by the prison guards, and it ends
with her, again like a queen, accompanied by her handsome youth, having to walk along all the corridors saying
hello to the prisoners one by one, shaking their hands
through the almost comical bars, which have yet to be
replaced by cell doors in this prison deep in the Portuguese provinces, and lastly having to be photographed
with the entire throng of prison guards who have en
route managed to forget their duty and responsibility
and have followed like sheep or little boys behind the
two, the queen and her prince consort, in a steadily
growing tail along the corridors of the prison. (And
there's also something about the light in Portugal that
suits her, liquid golden and at the same time clear, different to the light in Spain and undoubtedly caused by
the close proximity of the Atlantic Ocean, and then
something gentle and slightly melancholic, which can
also be heard in the language, the softness, rounded and
somewhat forbearing, a mood in conversations, in laughter and the nights, that also tallies with their love and
has the ring of its own termination, the impossible, passion as one long submissive sigh, when the last light is
sucked down and carried off on the surface of the water
flowing in the riverbed deep down beneath the yellow
overhang of rock on which the town was built and upon
which—seen from her perspective far below as she rides
into the dusk on the back of the almost black-brown

Arabian horse—it sits proudly aloft, and where the grub-
by kids and the washed ones and the washed ones'
mothers and a couple of the sisters and two of the brothers on their patched-up one-hundred-twenty-five-cc
motorbikes and some of the slightly older or at least
prematurely gone-to-seed men who always sit around on
the benches in the little park at the edge of the rock, are
crowded together behind the remains of the old fortress
wall, looking down at her as she rides alongside the river
deep down in the flat and endless lowlands, in silent
devotion, as if she is the sunset or is at least pulling it
along behind her like a smoldering thunder-red mare
into the night.) And then comes the morning when, in
bed in the girls' room—which on account of the visit has
been vacated and scrubbed and decorated as a modest
but fine bridal chamber with flowers and little bowls
with quivering water and candles on the little cement
windowsill in front of the also very little window, virtually just a peephole out to the adjacent passageway between the close-set buildings, and the girls, the
grandmother, and the youngest brother have moved into
the brothers' room, and the brothers are being put up by
various neighbors or with their wives at their parents-in-
law—she kisses his brow and in her clear, slightly tremu-
lous, almost strident aristocratic voice says to him that
she can't go on, it is far too overwhelming, all the attention, all these beautiful and fine and warm people, but
she doesn't know how she can do it, she simply has to get

a little away from it all with him, him, him. And later that day they take their leave, and the entire little town is in turmoil and distress, the young girls weep and the lati-fundiário, the mayor, and the patron have—in the case of the first two, for the first time in their lives—gone down into the very humble street in order to say farewell on behalf of the whole town, and she shakes the hands of the fine gentlemen and embraces the women and picks up the youngest little brother and weeps like them and promises that she will soon return, but they will never see her again.

The days and weeks in Lisbon, the clear, higher, harder light out here by the coast, the slightly forsaken hazi-ness of the city, a forgotten region of outermost Europe, the sound of the street-cleaning trucks advancing slowly through the streets behind Praça do Rossio in the last hour before daybreak, like big beetles snorting hoarsely in the dust of the strangely quiet city, which has a far from metropolitan sound, she who, wherever she is, is she who she is, and shows a new side of herself in every place, having drunk uma bica with the local men in the provincial town, standing at the metal countertop in front of black-and-white clad waiters in the café on the square, and along with the mothers, grandmothers, and older girls in the kitchens plucked headless chickens while the ones that were still alive ran around between her legs, here she speaks of aesthetics and art history and

Baudrillard's simulacrum with professors at the art academy and parties far into the night with her youth and his friends at the cafés in Bairro Alto, the professors pour her port in small crystal glasses they keep on a silver tray in the bookcase of their respective offices, and listen to her earnestly and stand up and walk around behind the desk and fetch a recently-published catalogue or a monograph about their work, and place it on the table in front of her and open it reverently, and she turns the pages slowly and looks attentively at each of the pictures, which despite the professors' exhaustive knowledge of the postmodern condition, of Lyotard, Michel Serres and Merleau-Ponty, are amazingly traditional paintings of Portuguese landscapes and café scenes with an occasional touch of the abstract or the expressionist. The young artist friends, who are part of the new era here and now ten years after the revolution, when money has just started to flow in from the wealthier Europe, and everything is suddenly opening up, and several of them or at least their slightly older colleagues, the ones who have moved on from the academy, have started earning money, good money, are rather more unrestrained, but also not completely free, or suddenly they can hear their own voices and keep catching themselves in perhaps not being (post)modern enough, provincial, they don't look straight at her, but are nonetheless forever glancing across at her, and when she suddenly quite naturally addresses them, they become instantly sober and ten years

younger and straighten up and nod, and the youth can
see their self-consciousness and laughs loudly at them
and slaps them on the shoulder and flings himself backward in his characteristic jerk that causes the chair to
crash and his pageboy hair to flounce, and laughs yet
again and yet louder. And all the while they keep an
eye on her glass and top it up and turn and shout to
the waiter telling him to bring another bottle or a cloth
so he can wipe the table in front of her, there, where
someone has accidentally ashed, they also find her somewhat mysterious and miraculous—not anything like the
Scandinavian interrail-girls in their cotton dresses, their
bare dusk-streaked legs and sneakers or espadrilles, or
one of the slightly older, single, unduly suntanned or
sunburnt women from Germany or Sweden who have
occasionally been brought along by people in their circle, and who have hung out with them for some nights or
weeks and drunk and danced with them and gone home
every morning with the man she had come with, and
then one night suddenly with a different one—but at the
same time there is an inevitability to it, that one fine day
she would be sitting at their table, because also here in
the capital city among the young artists, of whom many
come from families of artists and intellectuals or are sons
and daughters of the upper class of former aristocracy,
businesspeople and, not least, generals and colonels from
the days of military dictatorship, who have survived the
revolution and have continued living as if the twentieth

century hadn't taken place at all yet, even here, among his old friends, he is something very special, a sort of child of nature or uncontrollable genius like Caravaggio, who they, albeit he is one of the youngest, treat with the greatest of respect and from whom they expect the impossible, not just as a painter, but as a mythological figure who was sooner or later bound to return from a long journey with a woman who isn't even simply a model in Paris or a star from Hollywood, but a noble-woman straight out of one of the candelabra-lit rooms or castle terraces in *Barry Lyndon* (which at this very time is again showing in the Lisbon cinemas), a completely different era and a completely different world that has never existed.

Next moment they're back in the Danish provincial capi-tal, and "the endless summer" is to carry on as before, but it's as if it can't recognize itself or can't quite remem-ber how it went about it, as if in their absence time has suddenly started to pass, and the Portuguese light has merely been a glimmer of the impossible or hasn't been at all. And this is also when the girl and the slender, sensitive, and oh so fine boy part, but say that it is pre-cisely so as not to part, and she goes with the other one, the handsome one with the swaying arms and beautiful open and always empty hands, to America. But that's a different story, which obviously takes place at the same time as this one, because everything in this coursing tale

actually happens at the same time, but it will nonetheless be told at the end, in the cadence (as a final sigh),
because it is the one that harbors the definitive, unlike
this story of impossible love carrying on across separa-
tion and cessation and forever chiming in all of them,
continuing long after "the endless summer" is long since
over, across death, all this death that is to come.

So here he goes again, the beautiful Portuguese
youth, this mythological figure, walking down the street
in the Danish provincial capital, alone, defying everything—closed faces, self-contained, miserly Protestantism
that no longer has any god other than work, the endless
winter, darkness, snow that the moment it kisses the
asphalt is changed into slushy, mucky drifts along the
curb—wearing his olive-dust-glinting gentleman's coat,
the newly-greased light-brown leather ankle-boots, and
the hat, now no longer the "artist's hat" of "the endless
summer" at "the white farmhouse," but a classic gentleman's hat as worn by the patron from his hometown, head
held high and still occasionally dazzling the passersby
with his smile, his shoulder-length chestnut-brown hair,
which she occasionally cuts at the round dining table
in the little room on the fourth floor; but as the weeks,
months pass, and the winter doesn't seem to make any
progress or look like it will ever come to an end, the
slush soaks into the coattails as dull white-rimmed stains
on the previously so olive-dust-glinting, the boots can
no longer keep the slush out, they too get rims of the

salt used to de-ice the streets, the leather starts to crack, the hat loses its supreme patron shape, even the chestnut-glowing hair seems to be kind of splitting, his gait becomes increasingly stooped, with slightly hunched shoulders, no longer seeing Everything like he used to and having energy for Everyone and no longer suddenly exploding with the laughter that could usually cause even the most cautious and self-reliant to stop, against their will, in their tracks or at least turn their head as they left the bank or supermarket and look across at him and happen, against their will, to smile, not that he's starting to resemble them, he is still an exception, but more as an exotic and delicate, proud and beautiful animal captured and restlessly pacing back and forth or in tight circles on the slushy asphalt in a run-down provincial town's zoo. You should have seen him! she gushes, the girl's mother, now his wedded wife, she who had not for an instant throughout the entire honeymoon seen herself, now tells her daughter and the two young boys, the slender and the handsome, about the *sight* of him as he really is, unfolded to the full, in his own world. What you all see here is just a shadow! she says, thinking of him as he at this very moment, in the midday hour, enters the café on the square in his native Portuguese town, oh, if you only knew! she gushes shrilly, pressing her slim hands with their strong bones against her cheeks, tears brimming in her eyes, Stina! He was radiant! They idolized him, Stina, they did. And then abruptly sad: none of you will

ever see him like that, not here, Stina, I don't know how
he can live here, in this country, I can't do that to him, he
belongs down there, but I can't abandon my children, I
can't! she virtually whispers in the frailest of aristocratic
voices, thinking about the two little brothers.

But one day the impossible happens, the Danish provinces catch sight of him, all of a sudden he is taken in
from the cold and granted an exhibition, not at the
museum, that's true, or at the somewhat more modern
art house, nor at one of the few professional galleries in
town, but nonetheless a solo exhibition, in a bank, none
other than the head provincial office of Danske Bank
itself, ten paintings and graphic prints hung on the walls
behind the hard-working backs, clearly visible to all the
customers as the glass doors slide silently aside and they
enter. Now it is just a question of time, a few days, weeks,
then one of the customers will make a move, one of the
nouveau riche, yuppies, who have become aware of con-
temporary art and its investment potential, and buy the
first picture. The one will lead to the other, news spreads,
the local gallerists plus a couple of young international
comets from the capital will come visit, the second will
outbid the third, and the bank manager and curators
from the museum and art house and a number of the
younger trendsetting artists will look in, all doors will
suddenly open and "the endless summer" will stream in
and link them with the world and the time and give him

the name and the place in the social order that he sooner or later will need to have if he is really to be able to live his life here. As soon as the deputy manager, who is in charge of the bank's art association, has held his short speech for the guests and those few employees who are not duty-bound to pick up children, or are going out of town for the weekend (the bank manager is himself unfortunately unable to attend due to an unforeseen meeting in the capital), the Portuguese artist places his glass on a windowsill and walks toward the restroom and past it through a side entrance and vanishes. A few hours later, when the others, having spent time at a café where they have celebrated him in his absence, arrive home, he has gone to bed. For the next few days he does not leave the apartment, lies in bed until late afternoon, then he gets up, puts on trousers and a shirt and walks past the bathroom door without looking in the mirror and spends the rest of the day at the table in the sitting room gazing down at the tablecloth or leafing idly through some books or piles of old sketches. Suddenly one morning he has arisen before she wakes, has dressed and gone for a walk and doesn't return until late evening, and one night he doesn't come home at all. Next day they have their first argument, intensely, stridently, she suddenly looks like a woman approaching forty, she weeps, then they make love, intensely, loudly, and afterward they lie side by side with eyes open, shocked, lonely, and afraid of the future that until this moment has not existed at all. The telephone rings, it's the daughter asking if they should pop by. Not now, she says, perhaps tomorrow, replaces the receiver and goes back to the bed. Next morning the daughter and the two young boys drop in, and for a few hours they again sit as they used to, at the table in the sitting room, each cradling a cup of milky coffee, listening to music and not really saying anything. Suddenly he stands up and looks at the three young Danes, and they know that the time has come for it to happen. They put on coats, shoes, and boots, and just then the mother walks out of the bathroom with a towel wrapped tightly around her chest and another wound in a turban around her hair and she comes to a standstill and asks them where on earth they are going? On the way down the stairs, the girl shouts out, wait! but the other three just keep going, practically tumbling out and on down the street toward the town center, he is at the front in the middle and now without a hat, shoulder-length brown hair fluttering in the March wind, and behind him, one on each side, the handsome and the slender, like the guardian angels in *The Simple-Minded Murderer* accompanied by trumpets from Verdi's *Requiem* under a heavenly host of clouds rushing away from the final showdown they are hurrying toward, a showdown with the zeitgeist and the game they refuse to play, the oncoming random late-Monday-afternoon shoppers are brushed aside and left gawping like upturned pawns and gazing after them without grasping what is about to happen (and without, as is customary, grumbling or shouting, "look where you're going, will you, man!"), until they reach the bottom of the street and, just before the bridge over the railway track, turn in through the bank's main entrance, the doors giving a servile squeal as they draw back and make way for the supreme act that he, the artist with his fluttering hair and dashing olive-muddy coattails accompanied by his two guardian angels, without stopping, without even glancing at the employees—cashiers, clerks, deputy managers, and the bank manager who just happens to have come down from his office on the second floor and is standing in the middle of it all in conversation with one of the deputy managers, all of whom turn or look up in a moment of arrested time—and without respecting or even noticing the yellow security lines that mustn't be crossed, continue alongside the walls and while walking lift the first painting off the wall, then the next, and by the third the smile breaks out, and then, finally, he explodes in that overpowering laughter the world hasn't heard at all while the pictures have been hanging here, visible to all and sundry, but which will now return in the prodigy's supreme gesture and rejection of the game and its rules and the era in which it is being played, a showdown not just against the system of banks and money and the economy and the hierarchy, but with the entire culture it manifests, the nation, climate, human nature, not to mention the accursed endless winter, before anyone has stopped them, before anyone so much as shouts "stop!"

or "hey hey, wait a minute!" they have removed the last
of the ten paintings and prints from the walls and are on
their way back, in a fluttering of hair and laughter and
canvases flapping against the glass doors, which at that
very moment slide aside for the breathless, confused, and
yet again unjustly neglected girl, who has spent the last
hundred meters of street building up to her elegy and
now opens her mouth, but the moment she sees them
she suddenly understands everything and also just has
to give in and forgive, wait! she calls out, and romps
along behind them out into freedom, the real, supreme
freedom, the one beyond any order, out of this world,
out in the impossible, "the endless summer," where time
does not exist.

For the rest of the day and evening and long into the
night they listen to loud music and dance in the little
sitting room among the chairs and the paintings that are
leaning any-old-how against the walls, on the cupboard,
the windowsill, warped and scratched and retired from
the world. They drink wine and bake bread from the
last bag of flour, half a liter of milk, and the shriveled
remains of a box of raisins the girl finds behind the stack
of plates in the cupboard, the little brothers, who are
actually no longer that little, don't have to go to school
tomorrow, no matter which day it might turn out to be!
the mother gushes in her strident aristocratic voice, and
he explodes over and over in his all-embracing laughter

and falls back into the armchair and closes his eyes and spreads his beautiful fingers so the skin between them whitens, and laughs. "The endless summer" is back, and that's a fact, and of course it isn't, something has happened, for a moment they were out in the world, they had been cajoled or tempted, but had rebuffed it, brilliantly, that they had, but nonetheless now it exists, time, as a possibility, they can't stop themselves thinking, at any time, even here while they dance, in the explosion of laughter, in his toss of the head and backward jerk in the armchair and the crashing of the armchair and later, when they are lying in the darkness, in the throes of cannibalistic lust, in his bite and her bitten lips, and in her misty eyes, next morning when she steps out through the bedroom door and sees them, the girl and the two young boys and the little brothers, lying there in the sitting room on mattresses that overlap one another, asleep in the morning sun, yes, even there, in the tears in her eyes and the smile that breaks out, it exists, the future, all the things that can happen. It is not the bite in the apple that makes the Fall. It is the idea of a life after this one-and-only now.

It is spring, then summer, "the endless summer," they say, they name it as if invoking it, "the endless summer," as if it is language that creates the world, and not just a case of people being unable to exist without language. And one day in early June, or more likely late August, the girl packs her backpack for a trip to America with—not her slender, hypersensitive boyfriend, but the other one, handsome Lars with the swaying arms and beautiful empty hands. Yes, him. He's there too. What has actually befallen him during the summer? What has he done, has he amounted to anything? Has he at least made an attempt? Isn't he writing a poem? Does he talk about it? About being an actor, then? Well, yes, he does indeed. But does he do anything about it, does he attend a course? No. Doesn't he paint watercolors, make drawings, just a sketch? To be sure. But does he finish it? No? Girlfriends? Yes yes, he meets girls all the time, he does, beautiful girls, sensitive girls, easy, smart, cold, charming, crazy, calm, poetic girls, but it never amounts to anything with them, he gives up, they don't break up, it just doesn't go anywhere, or it dies out or comes to nothing, time finishes it off, just a couple of days is enough, and by then nothing has really come of it. All that's left is the smile, the lazy but always beautiful movements, the swaying arms, the open hands, this glow of a lifelong enjoyment, which is just a glow. In actual fact, he doesn't enjoy a single moment, nothing, it's all just resignation.

Departure to America: railway station: farewell to the others: the mother, the Portuguese painter, the slender, sensitive young boy who will never really look like a man, the two little brothers, the handsome one's little sister and, of course, the lanky Odense lad, we'll bring him along with the others into the railway station to wave goodbye to the America-bound travelers: she, the girl, wearing one of her big loose summer frocks, the chipped polish on her toenails, ribbon sandals and the long, sun-bleached, split hair, the slightly hysterical voice she has inherited from her mother, stooping under the weight of the cumbersome faded-blue backpack. And handsome Lars? He sets out, "as he is," he doesn't need anything else: his young body, simple clothes: jeans, T-shirt (white), a light knitted sweater tied loosely around his neck (the suntanned neck), the shapely feet (suntanned, the summer sand between his toes), a pair of ankle socks in a pair of sneakers, and that's it, a small backpack, the smallest, the most everyday, the practical Fjällräven (the type that most people use for an afternoon at the beach), and in it a windbreaker, an extra T-shirt, an extra pair of briefs (besides the ones he is of course wearing, even though they haven't been mentioned here), toothbrush, toothpaste, passport, visa, a wallet with a few hundred dollars, that's it, a person didn't need more than that as the twentieth century drew to its close.

Do they land in New York? They do indeed. Like you do. They're in New York, it's day one, he wants to go down to the Lee Strasberg Institute, gateway to the dream of being an actor, to Broadway and Hollywood, she'd like a wander first, Central Park, the Empire State Building, see a bit of it all. He can't be bothered, he wants to find the Strasberg Institute. She goes with him down to the Strasberg Institute. And then they're there, an old building in a side street, a scratched metal door, loads of young people walking in and out, perfectly ordinary young people carrying bags and small backpacks with their rehearsal clothes, most likely, scripts under their arms. No one he recognizes, no stars. Nothing happening. What had you imagined? she says. He doesn't know, be discovered, probably, he wants to be a movie actor. They're there for half an hour. Then they leave. What now? We've only just landed! she says. He sighs. They stay in New York for a week or two. Like you do. She sees a bit of it all, excited, overawed. He goes along with her. Or he spends a day at the hostel, lies in bed and looks at the ceiling. Then they move on. They don't rent a car (like you usually would) and drive across the continent to the Pacific coast. They do the trip by bus, Greyhound (like indeed you also would), but even by the time they get to Santa Barbara, where one or the other knows someone or other, they've started getting on one another's nerves, or more to the point: his indolence, which unlike hers is not pleasure-filled, gets on her nerves, that he can't be bothered to do anything, not even here in the New World where everything is possible and the sun is shining. She wants to go to the beach, see the Pacific! have a go at surfing! diving! meet new people! fall in love! What with? With the whole thing! He can't be bothered, he stays up by the house, all that exertion, first you have to get there, then get back. They part company, he hitches north, ends up in San Francisco, and that's where it happens. What?

He doesn't know who or what he is, for pity's sake. Isn't it enough simply to exist? All that stuff you absolutely have to try out. Why? What is it you have to find out or arrive at? He's right here, damn it. He closes his eyes, let it happen, once, okay, just the once. What? Back home on the island, in "the endless summer," he did of course smoke hash, once (it made him sleepy, even more lethargic, fall asleep), get drunk (made him melancholic, sentimental, pining, instead of dancing and letting himself go, gave up, didn't even give in, just slumped on a chair at the table, stuck his finger in the hot wax under the flame, withdrew his finger and let the wax dry on his fingertip and stared at it, the finger, the wax, rubbed it off and stuck his finger in the liquid wax under the flame, went off into a reverie, and so forth), of course he knows, he's intelligent, he's perfectly capable of seeing himself, he smiles, lazily, indolently, no end to his charm, after all, now he'll just give it a go with another man, just the once, it's not anything he's been thinking about for ages, not anything that has spent years of longing inside his flesh, "ah!" not anything he's had to hide throughout his entire boyhood and youth in the little provincial town with all its restrictive norms and rules, not recurring sighs at the sight of a tight boy-butt, not an irrepressible

frisson of desire to be able to say, uninhibitedly, coquett-
ishly, "hi, girls, so how are we today?!" when they meet in
the gay bar, after all, he's not "coming out," what happens
just happens, first option: he drifts around the streets, up
and down them he goes, the steep streets in the sun in
San Francisco, the narrow streets in the slightly older,
run-down, charming neighborhood with all the color-
fully painted houses, this atmosphere of the eternal hippie, time that can no longer be bothered to pass, it suits
him, he likes it, he sits for a while in the sun in front of a
café, or at the bar counter in the late afternoon, flickering
sunlight shining in through the windows, handsome as
he is, fair, the sun-bleached salty hair and the suntanned
limbs, the carelessness, laziness of his movements, which
here on the American West Coast suddenly seem pro-
vocatively nonchalant, coquettish, irresistible, first the
one, then a second, then a third guy comes over to him,
would he maybe like a drink or a freshly-squeezed juice,
"how are you doing?" and "where do you come from?"
he can't be bothered, he just smiles, laughs with a sigh,
this damned charming sexy breathy laughter, why, after
all, why not, they get talking, the evening draws in, it
gets dark, and the other guy suggests they go home to
his place, and that's what they do . . .

At some point, after a few weeks, months, he meets up
with the girl again, he can't be bothered any more, he
hasn't for a long time, he just hasn't made the effort to

go home (what's he meant to do there?). What he's been up to? Nothing, he's just drifted around a bit, in San Francisco, then later he hitches down the Pacific coast, is he in Los Angeles? Maybe, maybe not, does it really matter if he's in Los Angeles, loads of other people must be or have been there, lots of wide streets, people in their cars, Sunset Boulevard, but no loci, at least there were those in San Francisco, one day he was out at Malibu Beach, walked a little way up into the dry hills, pissed on a faded-green bush—or was it an agave?—turned around and looked out across the ocean, it looked like an ocean. At some point he meets up with the girl again, quite by chance actually, somewhere between Santa Barbara and Santa Monica, maybe, she's run out of money, or maybe it's time for her to go home, and so he goes with her.

They're back on the island, in "the endless summer," the girl euphoric, for weeks, months, with shiny dancing eyes and nonstop prattling, laughing, waving around her both chubby and long, both gracious and bungling fingers, always in motion, like tentacles on an insect, she is overflowing with stories, longs to be back, has crazy plans for her future in America, Mexico, South America, she's in love, as usual when traveling she's met the one, the love of her life, maybe she'll go back to him, live with the Mexican or Venezuelan or Colombian guy she presumably met on the beach, in Santa Barbara or Santa Monica, or maybe she's been all the way down to Baja

California, Yucatán? one of those suntanned idlers always drifting around like one of the more or less "locals"
on every beach around the world where the sand burns
under your feet, she was made for him and that life and
that *climate*, not Denmark, not the endless cold, slushy
winters, the grumpy people, she's a life-loving person, she
wants to live, dance, *enjoy* life, she almost can't wait, she's
just popped home to say hi, earn some money waiting
tables or tending bar, as soon as she's got enough money
she'll be off again, out! He, on the other hand, handsome
Lars, has nothing to tell, he can't be bothered, what is
he meant to say? America, well it's just . . . America. But
he looks a dream, they all say that, "Lars, you look like
the American dream!" Long-Beach-tanned, with sun-
bleached hair, those twinkling blue eyes, hasn't he been
discovered? Wasn't he going to Hollywood? Well, sure,
that was the plan, but he didn't really quite get there, or
maybe he did, he went to the Strasberg Institute, in New
York, but that was just a school. Right, well, they say, you
have to start somewhere, it's hard work, what had you
imagined? Nothing, that things would just happen; isn't
that what happens in America, it's there things happen,
isn't it? He smiles, resigned, charming, he knows what
he's like, but he can't be bothered ("know yourself," for
pity's sake!). He resigns himself to what there was, does
as he did before he left for what really was and turned
out to be the journey of his life (whereas for her it was
just one of the numerous trips with which she postponed

her life, and which thus ultimately became her destiny, her modus vivendum, the eternal deferment); nothing, that's what he does, unlike the girl he doesn't seem to have had any kind of significant or unforgettable experience, "the journey of my life," nothing happened.

Some weeks have passed, months, half a year, a whole year? Suddenly one evening the phone rings at the home of a young single woman and her daughter on the outskirts of an even smaller provincial town, almost just a one-horse backwater, in the southern periphery of the country, where it is at its extreme and utmost state of impoverishment, and where junkies, battered mopeds with green milk-crates on the luggage carrier, and human peculiarities are in the majority, and where the slender, sensitive young boy now lives in a rented basement room, which isn't really a room but just the inmost of a series of small damp cement rooms of the kind found under most of the run-down buildings from the mid-twentieth-century on the outskirts of market towns or one-horse backwaters, the kind of room that the owner has either never been down to visit or in the very first week filled to the low ceiling with odds and ends and half-emptied packing-cases brought along from earlier or even earlier lives, and a couple of shelves on the wall furthest away from the door perhaps hold some jars of now thoroughly slimy-brown preserved fruit, cucumber or pumpkin left by the previous or previous-but-one owner,

jars that can only just be made out in the grimy-ish light
seeping in through the little window, virtually just a
peephole, north-facing and with a greasy, cracked, and
sometimes simply smashed windowpane, stuck together
by two-, ten-, twenty-year-old remains of cobweb, and
in which the slender young boy has, for four hundred
kroner per month, been permitted to stay temporarily
with his growing despair, and down to which, with help
from the carpenter's assistant who is currently the boyfriend of the single mother upstairs, he has dragged an
old wood-burning stove that he has "borrowed" from
one of the many sheds or charming little half-timbered
buildings dotted along the forest tracks and under the
administration of the manor house, the location of which
is a mystery to him, and installed (the stove) by simply taking a claw hammer and knocking a hole in the
chimney and shoving the stovepipe in and then closing
the hole with mineral wool insulation and mortar, and
to which he now returns "home" every evening at dusk
from the experimental drama school, by means of which
he is currently attempting to come into existence, lights
the wood-burner with twigs he has found on his walk
through the forest, and maybe a log "borrowed" from
one of the nearest neighbors' carports, and then sits for
an hour or two in the soporific rumbling of the flames
in the stove and yet again fails in the writing of a poem,
gives up, snuffs out the candle and lies down on the
mattress on the floor and pulls the smoke-greasy duvet

over the suede jacket and the cap he keeps on around the
clock all through the winter. The single mother opens
the hatch placed under the back staircase that leads up
to the second floor, takes a few steps down the ladder
and calls out to him. He gets up from the little table in
front of the stove, unravels the duvet he had wrapped
around himself like a thick floor-length skirt before sitting down, and opens the door and says, yes? Phone for
you, she says. For me? he says. Yes. And so he ascends the
stairs, steps out of his winter boots and walks into the
room in his thick woolen socks and picks up the receiver
from the table where the telephone is sitting. Hello?
he says. He can hear it straight away in the voice. The
slightly strident, aristocratic female voice that has always
sounded as if it was singing the final terribly beautiful
song of a dying aristocracy, but now finally cracks. Have
you heard?! she says. What? he says. He hasn't heard
anything, he knows nothing about the world beyond
his own despair and basement room with the stove and
its red-hot chinks, several months have passed since he
spoke with anyone other than the single mother upstairs,
her daughter, and the carpenter, who is gradually moving
in, he hasn't even been in touch with them, the others
from the journey through "the endless summer." Lars . . . ,
she says stridently, raspingly. What? he says. He is . . . he
has been . . . diagnosed with . . . (and then she says the
unmentionable, the three capital letters that sooner or
later will turn into four, and which along with the threat

of nuclear war and its subsequent "nuclear winter" is their epoch's Hell writ large on earth). And here, at this very moment, in those three letters of the alphabet, or at least in the silence that follows them, "the endless summer" is finally over. Were there a Grace, a God, or just an Olympian narrator, then the tale would end here. But the worst thing about death is not that it is the master of time and the world of humankind and their stories. The worst thing is that it's vain, a pampered hussy who gets everything she points at, but is still never satisfied, she doesn't just want more, she wants to flaunt herself, show how wonderfully unpredictable she is, how impulsive, capricious, so eminently *alive*: sometimes she stretches, death, indolently, tenderly, ah! We've already spotted her, suddenly there she is, the time has come, but she drags it out a bit, upsidaisy! a moment more, a few hours, weeks, months, years, ah! she can't quite decide, now or . . . now? no, wait! maybe . . . You just never know with death, but once you've caught sight of her and realized that she's what it's all about, then you can't take your eyes off her, it's impossible to turn away or really concentrate on anything else, you're mesmerized, suffering euphorically, like being so intensely in love, seduced by the Other, until the moment she finally, suddenly, whoops! gets down to it or just, oopsie! out it slips, that little liberating "curtains."

They say he will have to fight, he will have to hold out, there are lots of people who live for many years with that disease, which isn't actually a real disease, he isn't sick at all, is he, what he's carrying around inside is really just the *possibility* of a disease, it hasn't developed, maybe it never will, or not for a few years, maybe many, as long as he has the motivation. But he doesn't, motivation for what? Just to live, survive? Do it themselves, they can, if it's meant to be so fantastic, seven billion people, all just surviving, fighting, holding out, for pity's sake, that's just too ridiculous. Handsome Lars resigns himself, smiles, he can see himself, after all, he smiles for a moment (his damned charming, indolent, and infernally provocative smile). Then the smile sinks, he looks sad now, not sick, just sad, can't be bothered to smile. After a few months the disease develops, first he just has a cold, maybe it lasts a bit longer (well it's winter, after all), then the cold turns into pneumonia, but it's not pneumonia, the doctor says, it's *it*. He is momentarily flooded with a cold light. Then he closes his eyes and lets himself ebb. It is perfectly simple. He wants to go home.

On a quite ordinary gray, blustery autumn or spring day, the slender boy pays a visit to the small detached house on the outskirts of the provincial town where the other one grew up once upon a time. It's afternoon, the handsome one, whose movements are now not indolent, but slack, is home alone. The little sister has moved, several years ago, the father is undoubtedly at work, at least he's not to be seen, perhaps he's just too hard to spot in the dimness of the house, built at the time of the oil crisis, with its much too small windows, some closed, with leaded densely-colored fluted panes through which the light can but sluggishly filter. The most present Third Party is the mother, who died a few years earlier from cancer, of course, the typical suburban death, after a long painful sickness, and who for her entire life (or at least the entire childhood that the once so handsome boy can remember) seen from the outside had been a quiet, gray existence, but seen from inside, in the dark daily round of the detached house, was always a slightly dissatisfied, hankering and, like the father, deeply Christian, that is to say bitter, person. The kitchen, murky, a bag of sliced sourdough rye bread on the brown plastic worktop next to the sink, a packet of sliced and stridently pink salami (the only color in the murky-brown haze), a small aluminum foil tray of liver pâté, lightly squeezed in the middle by the last person to have dug out a knob with his butter knife, probably the father, who has made his packed lunch in the morning and taken it with him to the office, and left the aluminum foil tray, the packet of bright pink salami slices with the white eczema-like spots, "31 slices," and the bag of bread out for his son, who can't be bothered, neither making a sandwich nor eating, he just can't be bothered, he's free, finally free from having to have an appetite for anything whatsoever. He sits at the kitchen table with his hands thrust in under the shrinking thighs, his bare feet dangling, he looks at the other, the slender one, with a resigned, now gently ironic smile. What they talk about we will never know, it's the silence we listen to, the ticking of the wall clock in the sitting room, the refrigerator that stops with a click and a sloshing sound, a car rolls past outside in the cul-de-sac. The handsome one sighs, he hears it, the smile rises for a moment, resigned, ironic, and not directed at anyone, and dwindles and is gone before the slender one has time to look up and take it in.

There is nothing more to be said, the slender young boy returns to his basement, which he leaves some weeks later in favor of a small three-room sublet in the capital, where he lives without contact to the surrounding world, no telephone, apart from the entry phone, which no one ever uses except, on a Wednesday or Saturday, foreigners delivering advertising brochures door to door, and where he sits all day long and long after darkness has fallen at a small table by the window with a view of the night sky and the ascending airplanes flashing red and white. "The endless summer," the girl, who sooner or later was bound to get pregnant, her vacant gaze when she comes home from the clinic, the photograph he had taken of her on their trip south, through Paris and all the way down to Portugal's Algarve coast, naked at the top of the dune, huge, heavy, the belly, the shapeless breasts that seem to flow down across the sand, the sound when they return to the provincial town after a month away and step into the room they have rented: the clicking rain of thousands, tens of thousands of invisible, panic-stricken, starved fleas dancing up and down on the parquet floor; her best friend, who is soft, dark, and maternal, and whose boyfriends and later her fiancé—always immensely energetic and creative young or slightly older men—always leave her, but never for another woman, always for the first man in their life; the slender, oh so sensitive young boy, who himself gradually becomes aware of men looking at him, and the potential advantages, first on Rue des Archives in Paris and in the bars and clubs of the surrounding neighborhood, later in New York, at the Zone with its two stages, where anyone with an inclination or sufficient disinclination can step up, disrobe, and self-flagellate, video projections on the raw walls showing Californian bodybuilders, all Aryan-blue-eyed and with bleached hair, posing, and at the back, somewhat randomly like the remains of board partitioning around a construction site, a public pissoir or maybe the back of a bus shelter, the very *zone*, painted black with an entrance at both ends and nothing inside except a dim passage, which is either empty or, without warning, like after a silent nuclear-war alarm, packed to bursting point with male bodies, copulating deliriously, the explosion of humid heat, the sweet scent of secretions (sperm, saliva, sweat, and blood), the doors these looking eyes could open: to apartments in Greenwich Village, dinners at expensive restaurants in Soho, theater tickets and weekend trips "upstate." The tale isn't "larger than life," it's the only salvation of the times.

One early morning the entry phone buzzes and the slender boy rises from the mattress on the floor and walks drowsily across and without opening his eyes picks up the receiver and says he doesn't want any, slams down the receiver and goes back to the mattress and lies down, and the entry phone immediately buzzes again, and he gets up, now wide awake, aggressive, walks across, and picks up the receiver and says that he damn well doesn't want any advertising brochures, and a thin, somewhat alarmed voice says that it's not delivering advertising brochures but a private telegram.

When he enters the hospital room, several of the others are already there, not all of them, not the entire "endless summer" gathered one last time, not yet, we'll postpone that until the finale, when the organ strikes up, but the girl and a female friend—who has not hitherto played any role, but who now, at the last moment, considers herself entitled to enter the story and, by virtue of the fact that she has very recently embarked on her studies to be a doctor, stage-manage the entire drama around the deathbed, convene the relatives, whisper in their ears with the correct medical terms for what no one wants to know about because anyone can see that it is no longer of any use or significance to know something that without a sound, without a word, you can, whether you want to or not, simply see, and hold them back if they instinctively reach out to touch—the handsome one's little sister, the lanky artist, who has not yet met his God, and the mother, but without her two boys and without her husband, the Portuguese youth, we'll leave them out for now. First, the room: white, bare as a village church; and in the room: the living gathered around the incomprehensible, what is no longer narrative, but image, icon:

He lies or hovers as if weightless in a web of transparent tubes and wires attached to his skin with pins, plasters, cuffs, and, at the other end, flashing monitors and bags containing fluid and blood suspended from shiny metal stands, the handsome body with its beautiful hands transformed into a score of bones set out in a rickety pattern on a white cloth (no longer body, but a vacuum covered with transparent sallow-gray skin stretched out by the bones as if by the poles in a tent canvas), hands swollen blue-gray and at the very end of the ankle bone shafts hang two colossal black-blue club feet, the head isn't a head, but a cranium covered with vellum, the hollow uncannily alive eyes and the youth's tender stubble. He doesn't look like, he *is* the one he is, it is prosaic and suddenly obvious: Jesus on the cross is not God's son, but Everyman, the suffering human being nailed to his or her consciousness. He looks at them, from time to time the pains strike, like a veil pulled down over his eyes, then he looks at them again, and again this hint of a smile that is neither scornful nor mocking, but just resigned, the gifted individual who has allowed life, all the possibilities, slip out of his hands and knows it and regrets nothing, that's how it is, ecce homo, here I am, my own creation. They don't say anything, there's nothing left to say, the monitors are buzzing, the traffic keeps moving on the other side of the window panes, la circulation, not headed anywhere, just round and round in this one and only world, not a word, no sudden despair or a final biblical cry, "father, why hast thou forsaken me?!" No, he hasn't been forsaken by anyone, he is his own creation, étant donné, the last bit of a human being hanging in a bare white room.

Can it really be true? Does no one weep, whisper, do they not give one another a comforting hug, they have to! It's as if they are immobile, transformed into pillars of salt, as if in this final moment they have looked back and seen what no human being can bear to see.

Then, suddenly, the bells chime, the organ strikes up, and six men in dark suits carry the coffin out of the church, who are they? where do they come from? the father isn't one of them, he is walking behind the coffin next to the sister, wearing dark clothes and strangely impassive, just like them, the six dark-suited men of various ages, men who have not been mentioned with a single word, but must have been there all along, beyond the language, on the outskirts of the story, like distant relatives he has never mentioned because they were nothing to him, because he wasn't in touch with them and couldn't see why he ever should be, but all the same they have of course been there all the *time*, beyond "the endless summer" they have lived their lives with wives, mothers, sons, and daughters, and now suddenly, at the final and exactly right moment, they have entered the story and have commandeered the coffin and are carrying it out of God's house, out under the low wind-swept February sky, along the bare, slightly sloping churchyard's crunching gravel paths in a straight line toward the hole in the ground, that's his spot. They stop, secure the ropes, and lower the coffin onto the joists, without a word and still just as impassive, almost professional, as if they aren't anything other than what they are doing at this very moment. Then the six men brush the grime from their hands, take a step backward and make room for the pastor. He hasn't said anything yet, just the words of the Bible, as if there had been an advance request for no form of personal reference, just the basic necessity, thank you, the ritual: "Earth to earth, ashes to ashes, dust to dust. In sure and certain hope of glorious resurrection, through the Lord, unto eternal life." The pastor says the last bit in a slightly quieter voice, as if it's impossible to believe, but has to be said according to the book. The father is standing behind him, and at his side the sister, the father doesn't touch her, doesn't even take her hand, she is totally alone, little shivers run through her, she tries to hold back the tears, she knows that she shouldn't weep, but she can't stop herself, she *wants* to weep. Around them, behind the dark-suited backs are the wives, a couple of grown-up daughters, no children; and slightly farther away again, standing in their own little group, like some kind of audience that doesn't actually have any business here: the girl, the mother, and her Portuguese husband, the two little brothers, the slender, sensitive young boy, the female friend, and the lanky artist. None of them live on the island any more, it is a "desert" or a "deserted" island, the handsome boy was the only one left, or rather, the only one who went back, not to retrieve, but to give up, and it really was like a homecoming for him, as if that was what he had longed for all the time, all the way through "the endless summer" too: to come home, home to the dark little detached house, the—after the mother's cancer-death—deserted, empty house, where the father lurked like a ghost, the definitively hopeless place, the terminus, to which all routes lead: death, he could finally surrender himself to it, uninhibitedly, brazenly, not just to death, but to that which is worse, the most rigorous of all taboos: to crave it, at last he didn't have to live up to life any longer, life's gift, his handsome body with all its possibilities, all its potential life, all the things he could do and ought to do with that gift of being born in the best, the safest, the richest, the most open of all worlds, and, what's more, with the ideal body, a body that would be able to learn everything, a mind and an intelligence that would be able to think out the unthinkable, perhaps, yes, just think! No, he couldn't be bothered, he had just one wish: to come home, home in the humdrum, the empty, the hopeless, home. Neither the dark-suited nor their wives have said hello to this bunch of godless strangers, not so much as looked at them, as if they are unwanted, accomplices in the shame that has been drawn down upon the family, only the sister occasionally turns her head and glances at them, quickly, as an entreaty. They are freezing cold, the February wind catches hold of their hair and the Portuguese artist's olive-dust coat, tears at it, thrashes with it. Twenty, maybe thirty years later they're still around, spread across the world like vestiges, residues of life, the kind that can be wound up in a single crumpled sentence, but which can in fact take several decades to get rid of. The girl and the sensitive, slender boy who across the years, and every time they return from each their travels and each their adventures with other, unfamiliar or far too proximate genders, have kept on meeting up and resuming something that is long since over, in the way young people still find it difficult to let go of what has been, because it was so short and it can't be true that it's already over, it has to last forever, we think and say to one another "till death do us part," we say, and it's not until much later that we realize it isn't just young people and the first falling in love, but love and life that are already over in the here and now to which you abandon yourself and in which you momentarily vanish, and that both love and life, just like God, are something we create after it, the miracle, has occurred, once it's over, that's when it comes into existence in the tale. "Earth to earth, ashes to ashes, dust to dust. In sure and certain hope of glorious resurrection, through the Lord, unto eternal life." The ritual is over, the soil has been thrown on the coffin, and the six dark-suited men walk in front of their wives, sisters, and daughters, and with the pastor as a sort of intermediary between the believers and the godless bereaved from "the endless summer," across the churchyard toward the parish hall, silent, purposeful, as if the waiting post-funeral reception is also a part of the ritual, something that (according to the book) has to be done not to guide the bereaved through their grief and give it structure, but as the triumph of the believers.

The parish hall, a mausoleum to the nineteen-fifties with dark paneling, long tables and varnished benches like a community center. The dark-suited men sit with their families and the pastor at the one long table, shoulder to shoulder and backs to the survivors of "the endless summer," who are also uninvited guests here, spread along the other table, too many to vanish, too few to form a community. No one says anything, it's a funeral feast bereft of the feast, no redemption, just the meek clinking of china cups on saucers and the blackness of the grave replicated in the coffee, reflecting the faces of the believers, pale and serious, but not from grief, on the contrary, in the triumph of the faith, dry and taut, like the faces in Bergman's least dramatic, most oppressive films, which are also the humble, the most sparing, just the fundamentally requisite, a man, a woman, a bare church interior, the gray light from yet another gray day outside. Just once, the sister turns and casts a quick disconsolate glance at the godless sitting around the other table, and the mother smiles sadly to her, and the sister looks down. The father on her one side, the pastor on the other, not a word is spoken, the father just sits staring down into his cup. Now what? It's as if the ritual has ground to a halt, the silence is no longer that of the faith, but of emptiness, an abyss opening up. First the one and then the other of the dark-suited men leans slightly forward and looks discreetly along the table toward the father, but the father doesn't react, and the pastor makes no move to shoulder the responsibility. At length, a young man stands up, one of the dark-suited, a cousin to the handsome boy, he strikes a single "clink" with his teaspoon on the coffee cup, clears his throat in the silence that was already there, and speaks. He says that death is God's punishment of the sinful, that nothing is meaningless, that disease, every disease, is a warning, and death is never unjust, no matter how early it occurs, it always has a message, and thus this day is not a day of mourning but of affirmation and proof that God, the Almighty, looks down upon us and weighs our words and our deeds, and that some people's lives are an insult, not just to life and creation, but to Him. Then he sits down, the last word has been said, and "the endless summer" is definitively over.

But in the silence, the tale fades away, in defiance and as preposterous as love it follows the bereaved out into the emptiness: the two little brothers whose father, the so-called "stepfather," had suddenly disappeared leaving them fatherless or that which is worse, with a displaced and humiliated father, whose nasal, bitter voice they will still occasionally hear, on the telephone and during sporadic weekends staying with him in the little low-ceilinged wing of his older brother's farmhouse, the nasal, bitter voice that within a few years will eat him up, the bitterness will become the cancer that bitterness is, a quiet fretting of the flesh, and before anyone knows it, and before he turns fifty, he's dead, and nothing will be left, not a commemorative plaque, not a mitigating word, just this merciless sentence, and then, perhaps, a consideration of them, the two little brothers, "he was their father, after all." And the lanky artist, he who will meet his God, will put every idea of art behind him and return home to the island of his birth, not in order, like handsome Lars, to abandon himself to his own death, but in order, like a true Christian, to abandon himself to someone else's and accompany his mother on the last steps along the path home to the Lord, never to return to life and the two little children in the capital city, but quite simply to remain living with his father in the half-empty, dark, and by now very run-down small detached house on the outskirts of the provincial town. Every Monday, in the late afternoon, these two elderly widowers of the same woman will be seen stepping out of the scullery door and disappearing into the carport and a moment later they reverse out in the now also quite run-down and no longer particularly cheap-to-run car and drive together to the nearest supermarket and do the shopping for yet another week. At an age of forty-seven or -eight, he will all of a sudden, like a belated Joseph, decide to take an apprenticeship as a carpenter, and subsequently the now seventy- or eighty-year-old parents of his old school friends, who had already left home several decades ago and have made a career in the capital city or abroad or have at least established a little nuclear family in the adjoining neighborhood with a small detached house, car, wife, children, and perhaps even grandchildren, every afternoon, when they're out walking the dog, will see this barely fifty-year-old apprentice carpenter and widower of his mother in his faded-brown workwear, and with the traditional folding ruler wobbling back and forth in his thigh pocket, bent over the handlebars of his father's old gentleman's bicycle like a scrawny secretary bird or the cadaver of a heron tramping its way from the vale and up the hill toward the residential neighborhood. At that point in time, he has long since lost contact with the rest of the survivors from "the endless summer," and the only friend from his adolescence that he still occasionally sees is the other once-so-obviously talented of the neighborhood's gang of hopeful sensitive budding artists, a son of a university lecturer, who, just like the lanky Twiggy one, had already displayed an amazing talent for drawing at the age of ten, and by his early teens was responsible for all the illustrations in the school magazine, which he also helped to edit and for which he wrote articles, while also being, one is here tempted to say *of course*, one of the most gifted in his grade and, again *of course*, played the piano, both Bach and Beethoven, sight-reading, improvisations, and his own little compositions, and, at the same time he was, *of course*, goalkeeper for the football team, the first team, and one of the three players who for the first time ever in the island's or at least the club's history brought home the cup from the boys' national table tennis championship; no sooner had he started at the senior school in town before his first feature article appeared in the local newspaper and simultaneously a long lyrical account—"The Evening of Multiple Emotions"—of the first school party appeared in the student magazine, and at the age of just sixteen or seventeen he made his debut as a poet in the leading journal of poetry in the land. Just like the lanky one, and possibly to an even more

promising degree, he can become whatsoever he chooses, but no matter what that might be, it will without
doubt be something big. And at this very moment, when
all doors to the world are open at once and it is merely a
question of choosing the one (or ones) through which he
will make his entrance onto the world stage, his older
sister, an entirely charming and sensitive pale young
woman who is of course engaged to one of the school
principal's talented sons, starts hearing the sound of
every single ambulance siren or fire engine as a sign that
her beloved has been in an accident. Before long she is
being spotted wandering restlessly around the neighborhoods in a flowing nightdress, hair tangled, madness in
her eyes and in loud discussion with herself, until all of
a sudden, whoosh! and she's gone, and it's said she's
been put away in the secure unit, which evidently (the
daughter's fate, or maybe rumors about this fate in the
very small residential neighborhood) is a severe blow to
her father, the university lecturer, who is himself a sensitive person and at the annual parents' cup at the son's
table tennis club, which he, carrying the same winner
gene as his son but perhaps not the same obvious talent,
is *determined* to win every year, he always ends up losing
control, hammering the paddle into the table and bad-
mouthing his opponents, the other boys' fathers, all of
whom are self-possessed citizens with jobs in banks, the
municipal authority, or smallish companies, until the son,
at the musical climax, both entreating and gentle, must

first lead his trembling and heavily sweating father to the locker room (to cool down) and then, helped by one of the self-possessed fathers and his rather firm grip on the father's arm, is assisted down to the parking lot to the car, which, however, on the advice of the assisting father, who is most resolutely of the opinion that the university lecturer is probably still too affected (indeed intoxicated by fury) to be able to drive a car in a responsible manner, they opt to leave there, whereupon they, the son still only wearing his club shirt and short blue table tennis shorts, walk homeward in silence through the quiet residential roads. A few weeks after the daughter's admission to the secure unit, the university lecturer also starts arguing loudly and publicly with himself, and it is not long before, for the first time in the history of the provincial hospital, the journals show that father and daughter are both in the secure unit, at the same time. From that day on, all the son's careers come to a standstill, as if all those wide open doors to all the bright futures on offer also slam shut in his face and lock him up in a vacuum or an afterlife he never puts into words, as if it was his own personal holocaust, after which it is no longer possible to write poems or create art. With due modesty, he commences a university course in literature, which he never finishes, but also never abandons, he becomes quite literally an "eternal student," lives for extended periods with his mother in the, like the lanky artist's childhood home, now very run-down and dark little detached house, or in a rented room or in small two-roomed apartments in the dullest neighborhoods of various towns. At the age of thirty, he at long last publishes his first and for the next twenty years only poetry collection, which is not, as you might otherwise have thought or at least hoped, a fervor of fate and frailty in the tradition of Sylvia Plath, Emily Dickinson, and Paul Celan, but instead just treats with and of the view from the window in front of his desk and the dust on the windowsill. He is no longer young and agile, but oldish, overweight, has a bald patch, and above all looks like an attendant, and that's exactly what he is: cloakroom attendant at the concert hall in the Broadcasting House or relief assistant in a small bookstore. Now and then, when he's home visiting his mother, he meets up with the lanky middle-aged apprentice carpenter, never "at home" with one or the other, always somewhere out in the, as in all detached house neighborhoods, strangely deserted public forum, in the dusk they can be seen pottering around the same quiet residential roads on which thirty or forty years ago they worked out their wild visions of other worlds, and they always end up on the same bench in the churchyard, where the lanky middle-aged apprentice carpenter as usual gets onto the message about the Grace of God and The Life Everlasting, but without ever convincing the other. And while they sit there (or before or after) and long after they have finally realized it's all over for them too, the once so alive young girl with the delicate bones and large soft breasts and the no longer just slender and sensitive but alarmingly emaciated one, yet to become the elderly woman who some day will be able to tell this story, will meet one last time, and at a churchyard again, of all places, but in the summer this time, and they will sit in the sun on one of the grass-covered graves, and she will say to him that in the photographs taken of her in the summer after "it" (the funeral? the child they never had?), black-and-white photos, her skin looked all gray, she'd got wrinkles, and her eyes were dead. And she, who could have made her mother a grandmother at the age of thirty-five or -six, will never have children, nor do the two little brothers have children; for many years, until she's in her late fifties, the aristocratic mother has no grandchildren, as if there is a curse on the family, decreeing that it will not be allowed to live on after them, and it is not until the youngest brother, who has been the wildest and darkest in temperament, passes the thirty mark—suddenly becoming deeply religious and marrying a woman from an evangelical Lutheran revival movement family—that a descendant is born, a little girl with a father who, unlike his own father, isn't paranoid and pitiful and full of hatred toward humankind, but, like the very same father, grim and determined with a dark glacial look in his eyes. And unlike the mother, who after the sixth of her seven possible lives, which she has lived under each of her six husband's surnames, reclaims the seventh time around

her maiden name under which she lives for the rest of
her days, the daughter elects to keep the surname she
just happens to have been given, which is neither her
father's name nor that of the tall fair man she spent her
many early years believing to be her father, but is the
name of one of the many fathers in her life with whom
she hasn't ever had anything in common, the man who,
what's more, had terrorized half her childhood, transformed it into a claustrophobic hell under detective sur-
veillance and turned her into a resident of Twin Peaks,
yes, the stepfather, the man with the gun, the pitiful one
himself, let us call him Mads. But maybe it's not her
choice, just yet another result of the indolence that for
the first decades was hedonistic, but gradually just became a dull resignation, in which she goes from having
been "the dark round and soft girl with the delicate
bones and big soft breasts" to being ever more disturb-
ingly overweight, albeit still animated and gesticulating,
as if there still was life. And whereas the mother, for each
of her seven lives, moves on to another astonishingly
idyllic or peculiar place, the daughter will stay put in the
small semi-dark apartment in a side street in one of the
more run-down neighborhoods of the capital city in one
of the buildings in which the stepfather's older brother
Buller had once invested his portion of the inheritance,
and into which in her early twenties she had been most
graciously allowed—by this stepfather's older brother,
who never condescended to speak to or with her directly,

but had his secretary reply to the humiliatingly humble letter, virtually a begging letter, the girl had sent him, a plea for just the tiniest little ground-floor or attic apartment, for which she would of course, like anyone else, pay the full rent, inclusive of electricity, gas, heating, and whatever extras might come on top, such as a rent increase in connection with "improvements" to the property—to move, temporarily, just a single girl's digs, a springboard before being launched into life itself with the husband who would prove to be the great love of her life, and with whom she would have her children, which she never gets, neither children, nor husband, nor any proper actual life, she will never get there, it gets stuck at the temporary point, the single girl's digs, the loneliness, the one quarter-finished training course after the other and the resulting more or less random and always short-lived temporary jobs, and all of it done under the same name, which she has fundamentally and from the very outset hated. When all is said and done, the Portuguese youth and his luminous, aristocratic wife—the two who, in the narrative folly, had briefly been king and queen—were the only ones in the godless bunch at the windswept churchyard who, as the pastor throws the three spoonfuls of soil onto the handsome boy's coffin, really understand that "the endless summer" is now over. Like a perfectly ordinary southern European man and a slightly older, somewhat emaciated, but still upright and dignified woman, they will rise from the table in the parish hall and a few weeks after the funeral they will part, and he will pack his belongings and travel back to Lisbon bearing the name that, in the narrative folly, he had given her and which seems to be the name of "the endless summer," and he will carry on his life there as if nothing has happened in the interim. And yet: they part, never to part, over the years they continue to send one another long passionate letters, and every time something terrible happens in one of their lives, or when on the contrary nothing has happened for far too long and life seems to have ground to a halt, in the middle of the night, when they are, each at their end of the continent, lying in the dark next to a new other and suddenly complete stranger, he or she has to slip silently out of bed and grab the telephone and with trembling hands ring the other, and they will talk for hours, weep, fall silent, and laugh, and the other woman and the other man, lying in the darkness behind them, suddenly wide awake and listening to this incredible passion, will feel dejected and devastated while also understanding that the pain they are feeling is not a humiliation, maybe not even caused by an abandonment, but what they are witnessing is something unique, something that only occurs once, not just in someone's life, but perhaps in the whole story, that these two unreasonably loving lovers are in a way also victims of the incredible, the exception, which revokes all regulations and is unreasonable, because it doesn't reason with anything else, it is indeed the exception, and something they just have to live with. But of course that is not humanly possible, there is no longer anyone who is that selfless. Sooner or later the younger, slender and slightly nervy Portuguese woman behind the artist's back will rise from the bed and walk out to the balcony with its view across Alfama and the Atlantic Ocean in the distance, and she will stand there for a moment in the darkness, silent and with a face that no longer expresses anything, and she will feel the warm breeze against her naked flesh before finally letting herself fall. And the somewhat older, self-assured and excruciatingly ordinary Danish man behind the aristocratic woman's back will be increasingly overcome by raging outbursts of jealousy, will stab quivering knives into the kitchen table and, under the strain, of course, out of his mind, will maybe even lash out at her, until one day she can no longer bear it, and despite his anger, his accusations, and his tearful entreaties, she quite calmly leaves him, packs her belongings and moves, first to a dilapidated sun-yellow farmhouse in a humid valley surrounded by bogs and nightingales some kilometers south of the provincial capital, later with the younger of the two little brothers to a small dark three-room apartment, and finally, once he, the youngest, has moved to the capital city in order to embark like his father before him on a training program in a bank, she settles in a modest townhouse on the Kattegat coast, where she spends her final years living alone with the lover who has, throughout the preceding six lives with six totally different men, loyally and silently accompanied her like a shadow: the stallion. And the young boy with whom it all began, this fine, slender and oh so sensitive boy, who was never going to strip naked with another man, never rub his skin against another man's skin, will finally understand the old woman he is, frail and mercurial as cobweb, almost just a voice now, a being beyond age, who has withdrawn from the times and lives as a shadow among strangers in the "City of Light," sits alone here in the high-ceilinged room in a neighborhood of nostalgia, her own muse, who has let go of the notion of a future, turned her back to it and, face to face with those who still are and those who will be, tells of that which has been lost and perhaps never existed until now.

And all the while, in the churchyard, lying under three spoonfuls of soil in his coffin at the bottom of the hole, the once so handsome boy. Here, the voice finally comes to rest and silence and can be reconciled, in death, which is the center of gravity to which it has constantly been drawn and wound its lines around: Earth to earth, ashes to ashes, dust to dust. In sure and certain hope of glorious resurrection, through the Word, unto eternal life.

Paris, April–June 2013

Madame Nielsen is a novelist, artist, performer, stage director and world history enactor, composer, chanteuse, and multi-gendered. Madame Nielsen is the author of numerous literary works, including a trilogy—*The Suicide Mission, The Sovereign,* and *Fall of the Great Satan*—and most recently, *The Endless Summer,* the "Bildungsroman" *The Invasion,* and *The Supreme Being.* Madame Nielsen is translated into nine languages and has received several literary prizes. The autobiographical novel *My Encounters with The Great Authors of our Nation* was published in 2013 under her boy's-name, Claus Beck-Nielsen, and was nominated for the Nordic Council Literature Prize in 2014.

Gaye Kynoch is a freelance translator of Danish into English, specializing in books and essays on various aspects of the arts, together with plays and works of fiction.

**OPEN
LETTER**

Inga Ābele (Latvia)
High Tide
Naja Marie Aidt (Denmark)
Rock, Paper, Scissors
Esther Allen et al. (ed.) (World)
*The Man Between: Michael Henry
    Heim & a Life in Translation*
Bae Suah (South Korea)
A Greater Music
Svetislav Basara (Serbia)
The Cyclist Conspiracy
Guðbergur Bergsson (Iceland)
Tómas Jónsson, Bestseller
Jean-Marie Blas de Roblès (World)
Island of Point Nemo
Can Xue (China)
Frontier
Vertical Motion
Lúcio Cardoso (Brazil)
Chronicle of the Murdered House
Sergio Chejfec (Argentina)
The Dark
My Two Worlds
The Planets
Eduardo Chirinos (Peru)
The Smoke of Distant Fires
Marguerite Duras (France)
Abahn Sabana David
L'Amour
The Sailor from Gibraltar
Mathias Énard (France)
Street of Thieves
Zone
Macedonio Fernández (Argentina)
The Museum of Eterna's Novel
Rubem Fonseca (Brazil)
The Taker & Other Stories
Rodrigo Fresán (Argentina)
The Invented Part

Juan Gelman (Argentina)
Dark Times Filled with Light
Georgi Gospodinov (Bulgaria)
The Physics of Sorrow
Arnon Grunberg (Netherlands)
Tirza
Hubert Haddad (France)
*Rochester Knockings:
    A Novel of the Fox Sisters*
Gail Hareven (Israel)
Lies, First Person
Angel Igov (Bulgaria)
A Short Tale of Shame
Ilya Ilf & Evgeny Petrov (Russia)
The Golden Calf
Zachary Karabashliev (Bulgaria)
18% Gray
Jan Kjærstad (Norway)
The Conqueror
The Discoverer
Josefine Klougart (Denmark)
One of Us Is Sleeping
Carlos Labbé (Chile)
Loquela
Navidad & Matanza
Jakov Lind (Austria)
Ergo
Landscape in Concrete
Andreas Maier (Germany)
Klausen
Lucio Mariani (Italy)
Traces of Time
Amanda Michalopoulou (Greece)
Why I Killed My Best Friend
Valerie Miles (World)
*A Thousand Forests in One Acorn:
    An Anthology of Spanish-
    Language Fiction*
Iben Mondrup (Denmark)
Justine

WWW.OPENLETTERBOOKS.ORG

**OPEN
LETTER**

WWW.OPENLETTERBOOKS.ORG